'Justin, what's the matter? Tell me about it.'

'I can't—so many things—there's no help for it now,' he answered.

'There's help for everything if you've got someone who really wants to help you,' she said. 'But how can I, if I don't understand?'

'How can you understand when I don't understand it myself?' he whispered. 'I want to ask why—I've always wanted that—but there's nobody to ask.'

She couldn't bear his agony. Without thinking about it, she leaned down and laid her lips tenderly over his.

'It's going to be all right,' she whispered. 'I'm going to make it all right.'

International bestselling author

LUCY GORDON

and
Mills & Boon® Tender Romance™
present
a brand-new mini-series

THE RINUCCI BROTHERS

Love, marriage...and a family reunited

The Rinucci brothers: some are related by blood,
some not—but Hope Rinucci thinks of all of them
as her sons.

Life has dealt each brother a different hand—
some are happy, some are troubled—
but all are handsome, attractive, successful men,
wherever they are in the world.

Meet Justin, Primo and Luke as they find love,
marriage—and each other...

Justin's story, *Wife and Mother Forever*:
on sale November 2005

Primo's story, *The Italian Boss's Agenda*:
on sale January 2006

Luke's story, *The Wedding Arrangement*:
on sale March 2006

WIFE AND
MOTHER FOREVER

BY
LUCY GORDON

MILLS & BOON®

First published in Great Britain 2005
Harlequin Mills & Boon Limited,
Eton House, 18-24 Paradise Road, Richmond, Surrey TW9 1SR

© Lucy Gordon 2005

ISBN 0 263 18747 0

Set in Times Roman 10½ on 12 pt.
07-0905-45302

Printed and bound in Great Britain
by Antony Rowe Ltd, Chippenham, Wiltshire

PROLOGUE

IT WAS four o'clock and almost time for Signora Rinucci's birthday celebration to begin. Gleaming black limousines were gliding up the hill to the Villa Rinucci in its place of eminence, overlooking the Bay of Naples.

The food and wine were laid out on the great terrace of the villa, best Neapolitan spaghetti and clams, fruit grown in the rich volcanic soil of Vesuvius, wine from the same place. A feast for the gods.

High above, the sky was the deepest blue. Far below, the blue was reflected in the bay, sparkling in the afternoon sun.

'A perfect day.' Toni Rinucci joined his wife on the terrace where she was looking down the hill, and laid his arm gently around her shoulder. 'Everything as it should be.'

He was a stocky man of sixty with grey hair and a heavy face that broke easily into a grin. As always, his eyes were tender as he gazed at his wife.

She was fifty-four but could have passed for her late forties. Her figure was still as slim as a girl's. Everything about her spoke of grace and elegance, not to mention marriage to a rich man who delighted in spending money on her.

Despite some inevitable lines, her face was still beautiful. Not pretty; it was too strong for that.

Her nose was large for a woman, slightly flattened at the bridge, dominating her features, speaking of character and decision.

Her mouth was wide and generous, and could break into a smile that many men had found breathtaking. She offered that smile to her husband now, her fingers caressing the diamonds at her throat.

'And your gift to me is the best ever,' she told him, 'as it is every year.'

'But it's not the gift you really want, is it?' he said softly. 'Do you think I don't know that?'

She seemed to give herself a little shake.

'That's all in the past, *caro* Toni. I don't dwell on it.'

He knew she didn't speak the truth. The secret that had lain between them for the thirty years of their marriage was as potent now as always. But, as always, she would not hurt him by saying that her happiness was incomplete. And, as always, he pretended to believe her.

Two men appeared in the doorway that led from the house to the terrace, and stopped at the sight of the couple holding each other tenderly.

Luke, the more heavily built of the two, grinned at the sight.

'There's no time for that, you two,' he said fondly. 'You have guests arriving in a minute.'

'Send them away,' Toni said, his eyes on his wife.

Primo, tall, with brilliant eyes and a laid-back air that proclaimed his Neapolitan ancestry, shook his head in mock despair.

'Incorrigible,' he told his brother. 'Maybe we should leave them alone and take everyone off to a nightclub.'

'You already spend too much time in nightclubs, my son,' Hope said, coming over to kiss Primo's cheek.

'A man needs a little innocent fun,' he said, giving her a beguiling smile.

'Hm!' She stood back and surveyed him tenderly. 'My

opinion of your 'innocence' is best not expressed at this moment.'

'No need,' he said wickedly. 'Not when you've expressed it so often before. I'm a lost case. Give up on me.'

'I never give up on any of my sons,' she said, adding softly, 'None of them.'

In the brief silence that followed Primo and Luke exchanged glances, each understanding the hidden meaning of those words.

'One day, Mamma,' Primo said gently.

'Yes, one day. One day he will be here. I know it in my heart, although I cannot tell how or when it will happen. But I will not die until he has come to me. Of that I am certain.'

Toni had drawn close to his wife in time to hear her last words.

'Cara,' he said gently, 'no sad thoughts today.'

'But I am not sad. I know that one day my son will find me. That can only make me happy. *Ah, there you are!*'

With a bright smile she turned away to greet the first guests. The newcomers had been ushered out on to the terrace by three young men whose facial resemblance proclaimed them kin.

'Mamma,' the tallest of the three called to her, indicating the guests, 'look who's here.'

This was Francesco, who might have been his mother's secret favourite, or might not. It was marvellous how many of her sons thought he alone was the possessor of the talisman.

The other two were Ruggiero and Carlo, the twin sons she had borne to Toni. At twenty-eight they were the youngest. Although not identical, they were much alike, both ridiculously handsome, with the same air of being ready for anything. Especially if it was a party.

And this was going to be the party of parties. As the light faded and the dark red sun plunged into the bay the lights came on in the Villa Rinucci and the guests streamed up the hill, bearing gifts for Hope Rinucci's fifty-fourth birthday.

Those present included everybody who was anybody in Naples, with a fair sprinkling of guests who had made the journey from Rome, or even as far away as Milan, for the Rinucci family was one of the more notable in Italy, with extensive connections in business and politics.

The woman at the centre of it was English, even after thirty years in Italy. Yet nobody would have mistaken her for an outsider. She was the heart of the family, not only to her husband but to the five men who called themselves her sons. Only three of them had actually been born to her, but, if challenged, the other two would have fiercely claimed her as their mother.

They were the best-looking men there: all in their prime, all strolling about with grace and unconscious arrogance. They were Rinuccis, even those who did not bear the name.

Throughout the evening Hope moved among her guests, receiving gifts and tributes with great charm, an undisputed queen among her admirers.

Not all the guests would have called themselves admirers. For each one who spoke of charm and generosity another could tell of ruthlessness. Yet even her enemies had not spurned her invitation.

The enemies were easy to spot, as Luke remarked wryly to Primo. They brought the most lavish gifts, showered her with the greatest praise and lingered the longest to say what a wonderful evening it had been.

But finally the last one departed, the staff had cleared the tables on the terrace and the family were free to relax with their various choice of nightcap.

'That's better,' Primo said, pouring himself a whisky. 'Shall I bring you something, Mamma? Mamma?'

She was looking out over the sea, and although her fingers touched the diamonds about her neck it was clear that she was oblivious to her surroundings.

'Couldn't she have forgotten him even today?' Primo sighed.

'Less today than at any other time,' Luke said. 'Don't forget that this was his birthday too.'

'Why can her five sons not be enough for her?' Carlo asked with a touch of wistfulness.

'Because she does not have five sons,' Toni said quietly. 'She has six, and even now she grieves for the one who was lost. She believes with all her heart that one day she will find him again.'

'Do you believe she'll get her wish?' Ruggiero asked.

Toni sighed helplessly. He had no answer.

CHAPTER ONE

'OK, FOLKS, that's it.'

The bell for the end of school sounded as Evie finished talking. Fifteen twelve-year-olds did a more or less controlled scramble, and in seconds the classroom was empty.

Evie rubbed her neck and stretched it a little to relieve the tension.

'Hard week?' asked a voice from the door. It was Debra, Deputy Head of the school, and the friend who'd asked her to help out for a term.

'Yup,' she replied. 'Mind you, I'm not complaining. They're good kids.'

'Do you have time for a drink?'

'Lead me to it.'

Later, as they sat on a pleasant terrace by the river, feeding scraps to the swans, Debra said in a carefully casual voice, 'You really like those youngsters, don't you?'

'Mm, some of them are smart, especially Mark Dane. He's got a true feel for languages. By the way, I didn't see him today.'

Debra groaned. 'That means he slipped away again. His truancy is getting serious.'

'Have you told his parents?'

'I've spoken to his father, who said very grimly that he'd 'deal with it'.'

Evie made a face. 'I don't like the sound of him.'

'No, I didn't take to him either. Too much assurance.

I gather he's a big man in industry, built it up himself, finger on a dozen pulses, everything under control.'

'And that includes his son?' Evie said sympathetically.

'I think it includes everything—you, me, Mark—'

'And the little mouse in the corner,' Evie said whimsically.

'Justin Dane wouldn't have a mouse,' Debra said at once. 'He'd hire a tiger to catch it. But enough of him.' She took a deep breath and said with an air of someone taking the plunge, 'Look, Evie, I had an ulterior motive in asking you out.'

'I was afraid you might,' Evie murmured. 'But don't spoil the moment. Seize it. Relish it.'

She leaned back on the wooden seat, one elegantly booted ankle crossed over the other knee. Her eyes were closed and she threw her head back, letting the late afternoon sun play on her face, where there was a blissful smile. With her boots and jeans, her slim figure and dark cropped hair, she might have been a boy. Or an urchin. Or anything but a twenty-nine-year-old schoolteacher.

'Evie,' Debra tried again in the special patient voice she kept for coping with her wayward friend.

'Skip it, Deb. I know what you're going to say, and I'm afraid the answer's no. One term I promised, because that's all I can do. It'll be over soon and then you won't see me for dust.'

'But the Head's knocked out by the way you've clicked with the pupils. He really wants you to stay.'

'Nope. I just filled in while the language teacher had her baby. She's had him now, a bonny, bouncing boy, which means it's time for me to go bouncing off into the sunset.'

'But she doesn't really want to return, and I have strict instructions to persuade you to stay on, full time.'

Evie's response to this was to back away along the bench with an alarmed little cry, like somebody fending off an evil spirit.

'What's up with you?' Debra demanded.

'You said the fatal words,' Evie accused her, wild-eyed.

'What fatal words?'

'Full time.'

'Stop fooling around,' Debra said, trying not to laugh.

Evie resumed her normal manner. 'I never do anything full time, you know that. I need change and variety.'

'But you said you like teaching.'

'I do—in small doses.'

'Yes, that's the story of your life, isn't it? Everything in small doses. A job here, a job there.'

Evie gave a grin that was wicked and delightful in equal measure.

'You mean I'm immature, don't you? At my age I ought to be ready to settle down to a nine-to-five job, one offspring and two-point-five husbands.'

'I think you mean that the other way around.'

'Do I? Well, whatever. The point is, you think I should be heading for a settled life, suitable for a woman approaching the big ''three''. Well, nuts to it! I live the way I want. Why can't people accept that?'

'Because we're all jealous,' Debra admitted with a grin. 'You've managed to stay free. No mortgage. No ties.'

'No husband.' Evie sighed with profound gratitude.

'I'm not sure that's something you should rejoice about.'

'It is from where I'm standing,' Evie assured her.

'Anyway, the point is that you just up and go when the mood suits you. I suppose that might be nice.'

'It *is* nice,' Evie said with a happy sigh. 'But as for no mortgage—what I pay on that motorbike is practically a mortgage.'

'Yes, but that was your choice. Nobody made you. I bet nobody's ever made you do anything in your life.'

Evie gave a chuckle. 'Some have tried. Not with much success, and never a second time, but they've tried.'

'Alec, David, Martin—' Debra recited.

'Who were they?' Evie asked innocently.

'Shame on you! How unkind to forget your lovers so soon!'

'They weren't lovers, they were jailers. They tried to trick me up the aisle, or soft soap me up the aisle, or haul me up the aisle. One of them even dared to set the date and tell me after.'

'Well, you made him regret it. The poor man was desperate because you'd kept him wondering long enough.'

'I didn't keep him wondering. I was trying to let him down gently. It just turned out to be a long way down. I never even wanted him to fall in love with me. I thought we were simply having a good time.'

'Is that what you're doing with Andrew?' Debra asked mischievously.

'I'm very fond of Andrew,' Evie said, looking up into the sky. 'He's nice.'

'I thought maybe you were in love with him.'

'I am—I think—sort of—maybe.'

'Any other woman would think he was a catch—good job, sweet nature, sense of humour. Plus you're in love with him, sort of, maybe.'

'But he's an accountant.' Evie sighed. 'Figures, books, tax returns—'

'That's not a crime.'

'He believes in *the proper way of doing things*,' Evie said in a tone of deepest gloom.

'You mean about—everything?'

Evie gave her a speaking look.

'One day,' Debra said, exasperated, 'I hope you'll fall hook, line and sinker for a man you can't have.'

'Why?' Evie asked, honestly baffled.

'It'll be a new experience for you.'

Evie chuckled. It was the happy, confident laugh of someone who had life 'sussed'. She had her job, translating books from French and Italian into English. She was free to travel and did so, often. She had all the male company she wanted, and female company too for, unlike many women who attracted love easily, she also had a gift for friendship with her own sex.

It wasn't immediately clear why people were drawn to her. Her face was charming but not outstandingly beautiful. Her nose tilted a little too much and her eyebrows were rather too heavy, adding a touch of drama to her otherwise perky features.

Perhaps it was something in the richness of her laugh, the way her face could light up as though the sun had risen, her air of having discovered a secret that she would gladly share with anyone who would laugh with her.

'Time I was going,' she said now. 'Sorry I couldn't help you, Deb.'

They strolled to the car park, where Debra got into her sedate saloon and Evie hopped on to her gleaming motorbike, settling the helmet on her head. A wave of her hand, and she was away.

She enjoyed riding through this pleasant suburb of outer London. Speed was fun, but dawdling through leafy roads was also fun.

Then she saw Mark Dane.

She recognised him from behind. It wasn't just the dark brown hair with the hint of russet. It was the fact that he was walking with his head down in a kind of dispirited slouch that, she now realised, she'd seen often before.

Mark had a bright, quick intelligence that pleased her. In class he was often the first to answer, the words tumbling over each other, sometimes at the expense of accuracy.

'Take it a bit slower and get it right,' she often told him, although she was pleased by his eagerness.

But out of class he seemed to collapse back into himself, often becoming surly.

No, she thought now. Unhappy.

She slowed down and tooted her horn. The boy turned swiftly, glaring, but then smiling as he recognised the goggled, helmeted figure pulling up beside him.

''lo, Miss Wharton.'

She uncovered her head. 'Hallo, Mark. Had a busy day?'

'Yes, I've been—' He stopped, reading the irony in her eyes and gave up. 'I didn't exactly come to school.'

'What did you do—exactly?'

He shrugged, implying that he neither remembered nor cared.

'It's not the first time you've played truant,' she said, trying not to sound like a nag.

Again the shrug.

'Where do you live?'

'Hanfield Avenue.'

'You've wandered quite a way. How are you going to get home?'

Shrug.

'Wanna lift?' She indicated the bike.

He beamed. 'Really?'

'As long as you wear this,' she said, removing her helmet.

He donned it eagerly and she checked that it was secure.

'But now you don't have a helmet,' he said.

'That's why I'm going to go very slowly and carefully. Now, get up behind and hold on to me tightly.'

When she felt him grip her she eased away from the kerb. It took half an hour to reach his home, which was in a prosperous, tree-lined street, full of detached houses that exuded wealth. She swung through the gates and up the drive to the front door, mentally preparing what she would say to Mark's parents, who would be home by now, and worried.

But the woman who opened the door looked too old to be his mother. Her eyes were like saucers as she saw his mode of transport.

'What on earth—?'

'Hallo, Lily,' Mark said, climbing off the bike.

'What do you mean, coming home at this hour? And on this thing?' She glanced sharply at Evie. 'And who are you?'

'This is Miss Wharton, a teacher from school,' Mark said quickly. 'Miss Wharton, this is Lily, my dad's housekeeper.'

'You'd better come in,' Lily said, eyeing Evie dubiously. 'Mark, your supper's in the kitchen.'

When she was in the hall Evie said quietly, 'Can I talk to Mark's parents?'

Lily waited until Mark was out of sight before saying, 'His mother's dead. His father won't be home for a while yet.'

'I'd like to wait for him.'

'It could be a very long wait. Mr Dane comes home at all hours, if he comes home at all.'

'What does he do that takes so long?'

'He takes over.'

'He does what?'

'He's in industry. Or rather, he owns an industry, and his industry owns other industries, and if he doesn't own them he takes them over. If he can't take them over he puts them out of business. That's his way. Get them before they get you. I've heard him say so.'

'So that's why he's not here,' Evie mused. 'After all, if you're busy taking over the world it wouldn't leave much time for other things.'

'That's right. I'm usually all that poor kid has, and I'm not enough. I do my best, but I'm no substitute for parents.' She checked herself, adding hastily, 'Don't tell Mr Dane that I said that.'

'I'm glad you did. But I won't tell him, I promise.'

'I'll make you some tea. The living room's through there.'

While she waited for the tea Evie looked around and understood what Debra had told her about Justin Dane, plus what Lily had just revealed. This was the home of a wealthy man. He could give his son everything, except the warmth of a welcome.

It dawned on her that there was something missing in the living room. She began to look more closely, but without success. She started again, examining every ledge and bookshelf, searching for some sign of Mark's mother. But there wasn't a single photograph, either of

her or her and her husband together: nothing to remind
her child that she had ever lived.

'*Who the hell are you?*'

The outraged voice from the doorway made her jump.

There was no doubt of the identity of the man standing there. If the hint of russet in his dark brown hair
hadn't proclaimed him Mark's father she would still
have known him from Debra's description.

Pride and assurance personified, she thought.
Everything under control. And when it wasn't he hit the
roof.

His lean face was set in harsh lines that looked dangerously permanent and there was a ferocity in his eyes
that she refused to let intimidate her.

'I'm Miss Wharton,' she said, determinedly pleasant.
'I teach languages at Mark's school.'

He made a wry face. 'Really!'

'Yes, really,' she said, nettled.

'Dressed like that?'

She looked down at her colourful outfit and shrugged.

'A verb conjugates exactly the same, however I'm
dressed, Mr Dane.'

'You look like some crazy student.'

'Thank you,' she said, giving him her best smile. She
knew he hadn't meant a compliment but she couldn't
resist riling him. 'At my age that's a really nice thing to
hear.'

'I wasn't flattering you.'

'You amaze me. I'd assumed you went through life
winning hearts with your diplomacy.'

There was a flicker in his eyes that suggested uncertainty. Was she, or wasn't she, daring to mock him?

Let him wonder, she thought.

'How old are you?' he demanded.

'Old enough not to tolerate being barked at.'

'All right, all right,' he said in the voice of a man making a concession. 'Maybe I was hasty. We'll start again.'

She stared at him in fascination. This man was so lacking in social skills that he was almost entertaining.

'I suppose that's as much of an apology as I'm going to get,' she observed.

'It wasn't meant as an apology. I'm not used to coming home and finding myself under investigation by strangers.'

'Investigation?'

'It's a politer word than spying. Are you here to report back to the social services? If so, tell them that my son has a good home and doesn't need anyone's interference.'

'I'm not sure I could say that,' she replied quietly.

'What?'

'Is this a good home? You tell me. What I've seen so far looks pretty bleak. Oh, it's comfortable enough, plenty of money spent. But after all, what's money?'

Now it was his turn to be fascinated. 'Some people think money amounts to quite a lot.'

'Not if it's all you have.'

'And you feel entitled to make that judgement, do you?'

'Why not? At least I looked at the whole room. You judged me on the basis of my clothes and my age.'

'I told you, I've drawn a line under that,' he said impatiently.

'But maybe I haven't,' she said, incensed again. 'And maybe I stand on my right to jump to conclusions, just like you.'

She knew she was treading on thin ice, but what the

hell? She was usually slow to anger, but there was something about this man that made her want to be unreasonable. In fact, there was something about him that made her want to jump up and down on his head.

He gave an exasperated sigh. 'This is getting us nowhere. What are you doing in my house?'

House, she noticed. Not home. Well, he was right about that.

'I gave Mark a lift.'

'Riding that contraption outside?'

'No,' she shot back. 'I rode it while he ran behind—' She checked herself. This was no time for sarcasm. 'Of course. He rode pillion.'

'Did he have a helmet?'

'Yes, I gave him mine.'

'So you rode without one?'

'Yes.'

'Which is against the law.'

'I'm aware of that, but what else could I do? Leave him there? The point is, his head was safe.'

'But yours wasn't.'

'I'm overwhelmed by your concern,' she snapped.

'My concern,' he snapped back, 'is for my son if you'd been stopped by the police while in breach of the law.'

Evie ground her teeth but wouldn't risk answering. He had a point. An unfair point, but still a point.

'And why were you giving him a lift anyway? Do you normally bring your pupils home from school?'

'I didn't bring him home from school. He played truant today, not for the first time.'

'Yes, I've heard about his behaviour before this.'

'What did you do?'

'I went to the school and talked with the Deputy Head.'

'No, I mean what did you do when you got home? Did you talk to Mark?'

'Of course I did. I told him to behave himself or there'd be trouble. I gather he didn't listen. All right, leave it to me. I'll deal with him.'

She stared, aghast.

'And just what do you mean by that?' she demanded.

'I mean I'll make sure he knows the consequences of disobeying me again. Isn't that what you came here for?'

'*No!*'

Evie spoke so loudly and emphatically that he was actually startled.

'That is *not* what I came here for,' she said firmly. 'That boy is very unhappy, and I'm trying to find out why. I hadn't been here five minutes before I could see the reason. Heavens, what a place!'

'What's the matter with it?' he demanded.

'It's like a museum. Full of things, but actually empty.'

He looked around at the expensive furnishing, then back at her. He was totally baffled.

'You call this empty?'

'It's empty of everything that matters—warmth, parents to greet him when he comes home.'

'His mother is dead,' Justin Dane said in a hard voice.

'She's worse than dead, Mr Dane. She's missing. Where are the pictures of her?'

'After what she did, I saw no need to keep them, much less put them on display.'

'But what about Mark? What would he have liked?'

She heard his sharp intake of breath before he said, 'You're trespassing on matters that do not concern you.'

'You're wrong,' she said firmly. 'I am Mark's teacher and I'm concerned about his welfare. Anything about him concerns me, especially his suffering.'

'What do you know about his suffering?'

'Only what he's trying to tell me without words. I rely on you to tell me the rest. What exactly did she do that entitles you to airbrush her out of existence?'

But he wouldn't explain, she could see. His face had closed against her.

It was her own fault, she realised. What had she been thinking of to have lost her temper?

She took some deep breaths and tried to calm down. He seemed to be doing much the same for there was a silence. Turning, she saw that he was at the window with his back to her.

He was a tall man, well over six foot, and leanly built with broad shoulders which were emphasised by the way he was standing. When he left the window and began to stride about the room she was struck by how graceless he was. There was strength there, muscle, power, but nothing gentle or yielding.

Heaven help the person who really gets on his wrong side, Evie thought. *He'd be pitiless. What kind of life does that poor child have?*

When he spoke it was with an exasperated sigh, suggesting that he was doing his best with this awkward woman, but it was very difficult.

'This is getting us nowhere,' he said. 'I accept that you came here with the best of intentions, and I'm glad to know about his misbehaviour. But your job is done now, and I suggest you leave it there.'

She lost her temper again. She couldn't help it. This man was a machine for making her angry.

'My job is not done as long as you're talking about

Mark's "misbehaviour". He is not misbehaving. His mother's dead, his father's trying to pretend she never existed. He is miserable, unhappy, wretched, lonely, and *that* should be your priority. Am I getting through?'

'Now look—'

A sound from the doorway made them both look, and see Mark. She wondered how long he'd been standing there, and how much he'd heard.

'Hallo, Dad.'

'Hallo, Mark. Has anyone offered Miss Wharton any tea?'

'Yes, Lily's made some.'

'Then I suggest you take it upstairs and show Miss Wharton your room. She'd like to see some of your interests.'

She guessed that he would really have liked to throw her out, but he would not do so in front of his son.

'Thank you,' she said. 'I appreciate your being so helpful.'

That annoyed him, she was glad to notice.

Mark's room turned out to contain all the gadgets any boy could want, including a music centre and computer. Evie guessed she was supposed to admire, and conclude that Mark had everything. Instead, she shivered.

Such a profusion of mechanical things, and nothing human. Even here, no pictures of the child's mother were on show.

'How powerful is your computer?' she asked.

He switched on and showed her. As she'd expected it was state of the art, linked to a high-speed Internet connection.

'It's the next generation,' he said. 'They aren't even in the shops yet, but Dad brought it home for me. He makes sure my machine is always ahead of the other kids' machines.'

'I'll bet your school loves him for that,' Evie observed wryly.

'At my last school they told him he was throwing everything out of kilter by making their computers look outdated. He replaced every machine in the entire school with the newest thing on the market. Then he turned to the headmistress and said, 'Not out of kilter now.' And he winked.'

'He *what*? Mark, I don't believe it. I shouldn't think your father knows how to wink.'

'He can sometimes. He says there are things any man can do if he has to.'

So, Evie reflected, winking was Justin Dane's idea of putting on the charm, something a man could do when he had to, but which was otherwise a waste of time. But she felt she was getting to know him now, and ventured to say, 'I'll bet he bought you a new computer too, and it was one step ahead of the school's.'

Mark grinned and nodded.

'What do you want to do when you leave school, Mark?'

'I'd like to do something with languages. Dad doesn't like it, but it's what I want.'

'Why isn't your father keen?'

'He says there's no money in it.'

'Well, that's true,' she agreed with a rueful grin.

'But I don't care about that,' he said eagerly. 'Languages take you into other people's minds, and different worlds, so you're not trapped any more, and—'

This was the boy she knew in class, words tumbling over each other in his joy at the glorious flame he'd discovered. Evie smiled encouragement.

'I like Italian best,' he said. 'One day I want to go to Italy—hang on.'

A knock at the door had signalled Lily's arrival with tea. While Mark was letting her in Evie looked at the shelf behind her chair and saw, with pleasure, how many books it contained. She took down the nearest volume and jumped as a photograph fell out from between the pages.

Picking it up, she saw that it was of a young woman with a little boy, plainly a much younger Mark. They were laughing directly into each other's eyes.

His mother, she thought.

Something caught in her throat at the feeling that blazed from that picture. If ever two people had loved each other it was these two. But she was dead, and now his life was lived with a harsh father in a house whose luxury couldn't hide its bleakness.

Suddenly she became aware of the silence and looked up to find Mark watching her, his face pale.

'Oh, that's what became of it,' he said. 'I was afraid I'd lost it.'

He held out his hand and she gave him the photograph.

'Is that—?'

'Shall I pour you some tea?' he asked, almost too politely.

His face was implacable, setting her at a distance. At that moment his likeness to his father was alarming.

'Thank you, I'd like some,' she said, recognising that she must back off.

He put the picture away and poured her tea, taking up their previous conversation about Italy, a country that he'd evidently studied closely.

'You've got the makings of a scholar,' she said at last.

'Don't let Dad hear you say that,' he warned. 'He'd hit the roof.'

'Yes, I suppose he would. I guess you need to be a bit older before you can stand up to him.'

'People can't often stand up to Dad. He just flattens them. Except you.' He gave a sigh of delight. 'You flattened him.'

'Mark,' she said, laughing, 'life is about a lot more than who flattens whom.' She couldn't resist adding, 'Whatever your father thinks.'

'Yeah, right,' he said, unconvinced. 'But it helps. And you're the only one who's ever flattened Dad.'

'Stop saying that,' she begged. 'And how much did you overhear, anyway?'

'Enough to know that you fla—'

'All right, all right,' she said hastily.

'Wish I could do it.'

Diplomatically she decided not to answer this.

'I have to be going,' she said.

'I wish you wouldn't. It's nice with you here.'

'I'll see you at school tomorrow. That is—' she added casually, 'if you're there.'

'I will be.'

'No more truanting?'

'Promise.'

They shook hands.

'Good,' said Justin from the door. 'The best deals are made over a handshake.'

There was nothing but calm approval in his voice, and she had no way of knowing if he'd heard his son's words.

'We've made a very good deal,' Evie assured him. 'Mark has promised me that he'll attend school every day from now on, and since I know he's a man of his word I consider the matter closed.'

Her eyes told Justin that if he was wise he'd better consider the matter closed too. She thought she detected a flicker of surprise in his expression, but all he said was, 'Mark, perhaps you'll show our guest out? Goodbye, Miss Wharton.'

He gave her a brief nod and walked away, depriving her of the chance to talk to him again. Which, she thought, had probably been the idea.

CHAPTER TWO

EVIE didn't teach Mark the next day, but she saw him at a distance and knew he was in school. On the following morning he was there in her class, quiet but attentive. As he left she drew him briefly aside.

'All right?' she asked briefly.

'Fine.'

'He didn't give you a hard time after I left?'

'He never said a word about my playing truant, but he asked a lot of questions about you.'

'What sort of questions?'

'About who you were, how much did I know about you, how were you different to the other teachers?' There was a touch of mischief in his voice as he added, 'I said you were no different from the others, and he said, 'You mean they *all* go around on motorbikes?'

She tried to suppress a chuckle and failed.

'You'd better run along,' she said hastily.

The rest of the week passed uneventfully. Mark attended every day, as he'd promised, and Evie was able to feel mildly satisfied for a job well done.

Her personal life was less tidy. Andrew was growing disgruntled at the feeling that he didn't come first with Evie. She knew she could save the relationship with a huge effort. But then what? Marriage, which she'd always avoided? Just how hard did she really want to try? She wished she knew the answer.

Tonight he was taking her to dinner and she had discarded jeans and boots in favour of an elegant blue dress and a necklace of filigree silver. She stayed at her desk for a couple of hours after school, catching up on paperwork until Andrew called for her. She was just finishing when Justin Dane walked into the classroom.

She could feel his anger before she saw it. It was like watching a volcano preparing to erupt.

'So much for deals,' were his first words.

'I beg your pardon?'

'You made a deal with my son, a young man of his word, according to you. He was to stop playing truant.'

'And he has. He's been here every day since. I've seen him.'

'Today?'

'Yes, this afternoon. In fact, he did a particularly good piece of translation. I've just finished marking it—here.'

She pulled the book out and showed him.

'Then where is Mark now?' he asked in a tight voice.

'He didn't come home?'

'No.'

'Perhaps he went out with friends?'

'He isn't allowed to just go off like that. Either Lily or I must know in advance.'

'Are you saying that he's wandering around alone?' she asked, horrified.

'I don't know. I wish I did. Where did you find him last time?'

She scratched her head. 'I know where it is but I didn't notice the name of the road.'

'OK, you can take me there.'

His casual way of giving her orders made her grind her teeth and say, 'Since you seem not to have noticed, I am about to go out on a date.'

'How could I have noticed?' he asked, puzzled.

'Because I'm dolled up,' she said, indicating her dress

and make-up. Unwisely, she added, 'I don't dress like this unless I have to.'

Incredibly his lips twitched. 'I believe you.'

'Mr Dane, I'm sure this will come as news to you, but I do have a life. I don't just sit here waiting for you to give me orders.'

'So you won't help me?'

'I didn't say that, but "please" would be good.'

'All right. Please. Now can we get going?'

She looked at her watch. Andrew would be here soon. She guessed how he'd feel if she put him off, but she couldn't shut out the memory of Mark's unhappy face and the miserable hunch of his shoulders.

'All right,' she said. 'But I don't have long, and I must make a call first.'

She dialled Andrew on her cellphone and was relieved when he answered.

'Darling, I'm going to be a little late,' she said. 'Can you leave it for an hour?'

She heard him sigh. 'An hour then.'

Justin's luxurious car was waiting in the school yard. For a while, on the journey, neither of them spoke. Evie remembered Mark saying that his father had asked a lot of questions about her. He'd described some of the questions, but how many others had there been?

She took a cautious look at Justin's profile, which was set and hard, otherwise she would have called it attractive, with a sharply defined nose and a firm chin. A good man to have on your side in a fight. Otherwise, steer clear.

'So, tell me everything that happened,' she said at last.

'I called home and asked to speak to Mark. Lily said he wasn't there and she didn't know where he was. Just like last time.'

'So you immediately blamed me.'

'I thought you might have some ideas.'

'I don't know why we're going back to this road,' she said. 'He's hardly likely to be there a second time.'

'Unless there's something nearby that attracts him. A cinema, a shop?'

'It's a tree-lined street. And so are all the others near it. What's the matter?'

She had noticed him grow suddenly alert, slowing the car and looking around him at the passing streets.

'I know this part,' he said. 'We used to live here.'

'When?'

'About three years ago. Is this where you saw him?'

'In the next road.'

He turned into the street where she had seen Mark slouching along, but, as she had feared, there was no sign of him.

'Where was your house?'

'Another five minutes,' he said tensely. 'The next turning, then the first on the right.' He was turning the car as he spoke.

'There he is,' Evie said quickly. 'In the cemetery.'

Of course, she thought. His mother must be buried here.

Justin was drawing over to the kerb and getting out. She hurried to catch up with him and together they climbed the few stone steps to the raised ground where the graves were laid out.

Something made the boy look round as they approached and it was Evie he saw first. His face brightened and he took a step towards her.

'Hallo, son,' Justin said.

The child checked himself before turning obediently to his father and there was nothing in his face but blankness. It was enough to stop Justin in his tracks. Evie clenched her hands, hoping he wouldn't berate his son, but he only turned away with a shrug that would have suggested helplessness in anyone else.

Evie took her chance, walking up to Mark and speaking quietly so that Justin couldn't hear.

'You know,' she said, trying not to sound too heavy, 'this isn't playing fair. You promised me, no more playing truant.'

'But I've been at school,' he said quickly.

'Don't split hairs. No truancy means no vanishing after school either. No forcing us to chase around after you, and sending your father grey-haired with worry.'

She thought she saw a smile of disbelief flicker across the child's face.

'I just like being here,' he said.

'Had you been here the other night, when I caught up with you?'

'Yes. It's beautiful.'

'Show me.'

He took her hand and led her deep into the cemetery, which was old-fashioned with elaborate Victorian graves and mausoleums. Grass and trees made the effect charming rather than bleak.

Once she looked over her shoulder and saw Justin standing where they had left him, at a distance, watching them, motionless, isolated.

They wandered on for a while.

'Your mother's dead, isn't she?' she asked.

A nod.

'And is she buried here?'

A shake of the head. Then, 'But she ought to be,' he said so quietly that she wondered if she had heard properly.

'What do you mean, Mark?'

'Nothing. I suppose we'd better go back to Dad.'

Justin was still standing in the same place, watching for their return. For a moment Evie had an impression of uncertainty, but that must be an illusion caused by the distance.

'Are you ready to come home?' he asked Mark as they neared.

Quickly he looked up at Evie. 'Are you coming with us?'

'I can't. I'm going out tonight and I'm late already.'

'*Please,*' he said.

Beside her she could sense Justin turn to stone, waiting for her reply.

'All right,' she said. 'But I can't stay for long.'

Mark's face broke into a smile of relief. Justin relaxed slightly.

'Let's go,' he said briefly, indicating the way back to the car.

Mark grabbed hold of her hand and almost dragged her along, making sure that she got into the back seat with him. Justin started up the car without a glance at them.

Nobody spoke during the journey. Mark kept hold of her hand and seemed content simply to have her there. Evie was glad of anything she could do for him, but she was beginning to be alarmed. This child barely knew her, except in class, yet he clung to her as though she were his saviour.

She didn't know what he wanted to be saved from, but the glimpse she'd had of his lonely life had filled her with dismay. And something told her there was worse to come.

Lily opened the front door for them.

'Miss Wharton's really hungry,' Mark said quickly.

'I'll go and see to supper,' she said, and vanished.

Mark gave a violent sneeze.

'I hope you haven't caught cold,' Evie said.

'I'm all right,' he said quickly, and vanished after Lily.

'I hope you can stay with us long enough for supper at least,' Justin murmured.

'I'd better make a phone call.'

Andrew's voice, when he answered, was revealing. It had a subdued exasperation that told her he'd been expecting this.

'I've got a situation here that I can't walk away from,' she pleaded.

'Another one?'

'Darling, that's not fair,' she said, and sensed Justin looking quickly at her. 'I didn't ask for this to happen—'

'You never do. Things just happen to you. Evie, did it ever occur to you that your life is too crowded? Maybe you need to junk a few things, starting with me.'

'You mean break up?' she asked, aghast.

'Isn't that where we're heading?'

'No, no,' she said frantically. 'I don't want to do that. Please, Andrew, it's too important to decide like this—'

'Sure, let's put it off for a while so that you can keep me dangling at your pleasure.'

'Is that really what I do?' she asked penitently.

'I can't believe that you really don't see it. C'mon, Evie, be brave. Say you don't care about me—'

'But I *do* care about you. It's just that tonight—please be patient. I'll call you again tomorrow, and maybe we can fix something—'

'Yes, sure we will. Anything you say.' The line clicked.

'Andrew—Andrew?'

She stared at the phone, trying to understand that dear, gentle Andrew had hung up on her.

'Did he give you a hard time?' Justin Dane asked.

'I can hardly blame him,' she said edgily. 'Wouldn't you be annoyed?'

'Probably. You sound as though you're leading him a merry dance.'

'You'd have hung up long ago,' she said.

But he surprised her by giving her an odd look and saying, 'Maybe not.'

She wasn't sure what he meant by that, but she had no time to brood on her own problems now. Only Mark mattered. She couldn't forget how he'd brightened at the sight of her, or how quickly he'd said she was hungry, an excuse to keep her here.

'All right,' Justin resumed in a businesslike tone. 'You're entitled to an explanation, so I'll make things clear.'

'Not now.'

He stared. 'What?'

'What Mark needs now is for us all to sit down to supper and be friendly—or at least act friendly. Explanations can come later. Then I'll tell you what I want to know.'

From his frown she guessed that this wasn't how people usually treated him. And she seemed to have the gift of reading his thoughts, for she could follow the lightning process by which he worked out how to turn this to advantage.

'Fine,' he said. 'Then if you'll have supper with Mark I can do some work.'

'No, you can have supper with us,' she said firmly. 'How often do you and he eat together?'

'Not often, but I have things to do.'

'Indeed you have, some more important than others. The most important is to be with your son.'

His lips tightened. 'Miss Wharton, I'm grateful for the trouble you're taking for Mark, but this is not your decision—'

'Oh, but it is. Let me make it clear to you how much my decision it is. If I can give up my evening for your son, so can you. Either you agree to be there for supper, or I'm leaving, right now. And you can explain my absence any way you like.'

Now he was really angry. 'I'm not in the habit of being dictated to, in my own home or anywhere else.'

She was too wise to answer. She merely followed her instincts and met his eyes. Anger met anger. Defiance met defiance. Mark, returning, found them like that.

'Lily says she's laid supper on the terrace,' he said. 'Shall I tell her you're coming?'

For a moment she thought Justin would refuse and walk out. But at last he smiled at his son.

'Fine,' he said. 'Lead the way.'

Mark instantly took Evie's hand and almost dragged her out on to the terrace overlooking the garden. It was a pleasant place with red flagstones and wooden railings, expensively designed to look rustic. Here a wooden table had been set for supper.

The meal was excellent—spaghetti, well cooked, expertly served; fish, coffee made to perfection.

'So, let's hear it,' Justin said to his son when Lily had left them. 'Why did you vanish tonight and worry everyone?'

'Oh, leave that until later,' Evie said before the boy could reply. 'Mark's the thoughtful type, like me.

Sometimes we like to have a little time on our own, away from the crowd. There's nothing wrong with that.'

'I only—' Justin began.

'I said "enough",' Evie interrupted him. She spoke lightly, determined to keep the atmosphere pleasant, but she knew Justin understood her meaning.

'I was telling your father about the last piece of work you did for me,' she told Mark. 'A really good translation.' She turned to Justin. 'He's one of my best students. You should be proud of him.'

'If you say he works hard, I am proud of him,' he replied.

She wanted to yell at him, *Try to sound as though you mean it. Say something nice without freezing, or sounding as though every word has to be wrung out of you.*

Instead, she said, 'According to his regular teachers there are other things to be proud of. They say Mark is always the first to volunteer, to help out. He's a good team player.'

Justin seemed a little taken aback by this, and Evie realised that being a good team player probably didn't rank high in his list of priorities. She was sure of it when he grunted, 'Well, I guess that can be useful too. What do you mean, his regular teachers? Aren't you regular?'

'No, I'm just a fill-in for one term. Then I'm back to my real job, translating books.'

'You're not staying?' Mark was crestfallen.

'I never stay long anywhere,' she admitted. 'I like to take off into the wide blue yonder. There's always new places to travel. I'll be going back to Italy before the end of the year.'

'Where?' he asked at once.

'Travelling all over, studying dialects.'

'But I thought they all spoke Italian.'

'They do, but the regions have their dialects which are almost like different languages.'

'How different?' he wanted to know.

'Well, if you wanted to say, "Strike while the iron's hot" in Italian, it would be, *"Battere il ferro quando 'e caldo"*. If you were Venetian you'd say, *"Bati fin chel fero xe caldo"*, and if you came from Naples you'd say, *"Vatte 'o 'fierro quann' 'e ccavero"*.'

'That's great!' Mark said, thrilled. 'All those different ways to say one thing.'

'But what's the point?' Justin asked. 'Why don't they all just speak Italian?'

'Because a regional dialect springs from the people,' Evie explained. 'It's part of their history, their personality. It's their heritage. Don't you care about your heritage?'

His reaction startled her. His face seemed to close, like the door of a tomb, she later thought. After a moment's black silence he said, 'I just think one language is more efficient.'

'Of course it's more efficient,' she conceded. 'But who wants to be efficient all the time? Sometimes it's more fun to be colourful.'

'I wouldn't get far running a business on that theory.'

'The Italians aren't a businesslike people, thank goodness,' she said, trying to lighten the atmosphere. 'They're delightful, and full of life and music. All those things matter too. Who wants to be efficient all the time?'

'I do,' he said simply.

Evie and Mark exchanged glances. Justin saw them but said nothing.

'Will you send me postcards from Italy?' Mark asked wistfully.

'Lots and lots of them, from everywhere.'

He began bombarding her with questions which she answered willingly. Justin seemed content to sit there and listen, except once when he said, 'Take a break from talking, Mark, and eat something.'

His tone was pleasant enough and Mark stopped to take a few mouthfuls. Evie took advantage of the moment to look around the garden, and saw a dog walking towards them, followed by five puppies, who seemed about six weeks old.

'That's Cindy,' Mark told her. 'She belongs to Lily. They all do. And there's Hank. He's their father.'

A large dog, part Alsatian and part something else, had appeared around the side of the house, accompanied by Lily bearing food bowls. She set them down on the terrace, returned to the kitchen and came back with more bowls. Under Evie's fascinated eyes the family converged on their supper, the five pups diving in vigorously.

They finished quickly, then looked around for more to eat. Cindy, evidently knowing the danger, had cleared her bowl fast. Hank seemed less well prepared, for some of his food was still there and the smallest pup advanced on him purposefully.

The huge dog began to snarl horribly, revealing terrible great teeth. Undeterred, the pup went on towards the bowl, while his father hurled warning after warning.

'Shouldn't we rescue that little creature?' Evie said, beginning to rise.

But Justin laid a hand on her arm, detaining her.

'Leave them,' he said. 'It's all right.'

'But Hank will devour the pup in one mouthful,' she protested.

'Nothing will happen,' he said. 'It never does.'

Reluctantly, she sat down and watched as the puppy, unimpressed by his father's belligerence, reached the bowl and tucked in.

At once the snarls stopped. Hank was left looking around with a puzzled expression as if asking what he was expected to do now.

Something in the huge animal's air of baffled pathos struck Evie as irresistibly funny and she began to laugh.

'That poor dog,' she choked. 'Beneath all the aggro he's just an old softy. Oh, dear—'

Waves of laughter swept her again.

'Come here, boy,' she said, holding out her hand. Hank came at once and sat gazing up at her, silently seeking sympathy.

'Poor fellow, you hardly had any supper,' she said, taking his face between her hands. 'Here, let's see if you like spaghetti. Yes, you do, don't you?'

She wrapped her arms around him, chuckling and kissing his forehead at the same time. Lily joined in her amusement, and so did Mark.

She glanced up at Justin, hoping that he too might be laughing. But he wasn't.

He was staring at her with a stunned expression on his face, like a man who'd been struck by lightning.

Lily intervened and hustled her little 'family' out of sight. Evie went to wash her hands where Hank had licked them, and returned to find Lily serving gateau and cream.

'You look ever so pretty tonight,' Mark ventured. 'You don't usually dress like that.'

'I was going out,' she told him.

'On a date?'

'Yes.'

'Have you got a boyfriend?'

'Yes,' she said, laughing.

'Mark,' Justin muttered through gritted teeth.

'Will he be mad at you?' Mark asked, undeterred.

'Nothing I can't handle,' she said cheerfully.

'I bet you could handle anyone. I bet you'd really tell him off.'

'If I did that he wouldn't be my boyfriend for very long,' she pointed out.

'Are you nuts about him?'

'Mark!' This time Justin covered his eyes and his voice betrayed only an agony of embarrassment. Evie almost liked him.

'That's a secret,' she said.

She was aware of Justin uncovering his eyes and looking at her, but she kept her attention on Mark.

'Is he nuts about you?' Mark persisted.

'He probably won't be after the way I stood him up tonight,' she said lightly.

'But if he's really nuts about—'

'Mark, that's enough,' Justin said edgily.

She noticed that the boy fell silent at once, as though a light had gone out inside him.

'I honestly don't mind,' she said. 'We're just joking.'

She gave Mark a reassuring smile and followed it with a broad wink. After a moment he winked back, then cast an uncertain glance at his father, as though worried about his reaction. Evie followed his look and was startled by Justin's expression. It vanished at once, and she supposed she might have been mistaken. But for a brief

moment he'd looked almost forlorn, like a child excluded from a charmed circle.

Absurd. Whatever this harsh man was, he wasn't
forlorn.

CHAPTER THREE

AS THE meal ended Lily came to say that Justin was
wanted on the phone. Guessing that he would now be
gone for some time, Evie agreed to Mark's suggestion
that they go to his room and, with a sudden burst of
inspiration, she signalled a question to Lily. Receiving
a nod in return, she scooped up a couple of puppies and
followed Mark upstairs.

Now he was more relaxed, chatting about the dogs
and what fun he had taking photographs of them.

'Can I see?' Evie asked at once.

Of course he owned the very latest state-of-the-art digital camera, and handled it like an expert.

'I'm green with envy.' She sighed. 'I can't work mine
and it's much simpler than yours.'

'It's easy,' he said innocently.

'Yeah, for some people!'

He giggled. 'Dad can't understand this one either. He
gets so mad.'

Mark switched on the computer and called up pictures
of the dogs. He had, apparently, taken dozens every day,
almost obsessively, reinforcing Evie's feeling that this
child lived inside himself far too much.

'Don't you have any pics of your friends?' she asked.

He shrugged uneasily. 'I haven't lived here long. I
don't know many people.'

'But you had a house nearby.'

'We moved when Mum left. Dad bought this place.

He said he never wanted to see that house again. And I changed schools.'

'Your mother left?'

'Yes, she went away and didn't come back. I've got some more pictures here—'

He opened another file of pictures of the puppies and she let the matter go, guessing this was his way of describing his mother's death.

There were so many pictures that it was hard to take in details of any one, but suddenly a collection of them caught her eye. Mark seemed to have taken them at the rate of one per second, so that it was like looking at a film strip.

He had caught his father at the moment when one of the pups had approached him and was ordered off. Undeterred, the little creature had scrambled up on to a sofa and made his way determinedly on to the desk.

Almost as though it was happening now, Evie found herself holding her breath against the moment when Justin angrily swept him off. But it hadn't happened. Instead he'd picked the puppy up in one hand, holding him before his face with a look of gentle resignation. It was the gentleness that particularly struck her.

Then he'd turned his head, seeming to become aware of his son and the camera. He'd held his captive out, clearly ordering that he be removed, and he'd almost been smiling.

She took a moment to study Justin's face. It wasn't handsome. The features were too irregular for that, the nose too large. Even in a milder mood he still gave the impression of power, and his dark eyes radiated an intensity that, she guessed, would put other men in the shade.

And women would be attracted to him, she knew. Not

herself, because he wasn't the kind of man that had ever appealed to her. Too impatient, too sure of himself, too unwilling to listen. She could imagine having some interesting fights with him, but not warming to him.

'Hey!' Mark said suddenly.

Startled, she glanced his way with a smile, and heard the click of the camera.

'Gotcha!' he said.

'Oi, cheeky!' she said, laughing outright, and he promptly snapped her again.

'Now look,' he said, opening the back of the camera and extracting a tiny card. He plugged this directly into the computer and the two pictures of Evie came up side by side on the screen.

'That's brilliant,' she breathed. 'Why doesn't it happen like that when I do it?'

Mark just grinned.

'Yes, I know,' she said ruefully. 'Some of us can, and some of us can't. They're beautiful, Mark.'

He took a small memory stick from a drawer, connected it to the back, copied the pictures on to it, and gave it to her.

'Just plug it into your machine when you get home,' he said.

'Thank you. I'll give you this back at school.'

This wasn't how she'd meant the conversation to go. She should be asking him why he kept vanishing and trying to understand him. But she felt that the key to understanding lay elsewhere. The friendly feeling they'd achieved would do him more good than all the talk in the world.

'Will your father cut up rough about tonight?' she asked gently. 'I imagine he's not easy to live with.'

'He's not so bad,' Mark said unexpectedly. 'He gets angry, but he's always sorry afterwards.'

This was the last thing she had expected to hear.

'He shouldn't get mad at all,' she said. 'Why can't he see that you're unhappy?'

He considered this with an oddly adult expression.

'He's unhappy too,' he said at last.

'About your mother?'

'I think so, but—there's lots of other stuff that he can't talk about. I used to hear him and Mum rowing—terrible things—she said he had something dark inside him, and why couldn't he talk about it? But he said talking wouldn't change anything, and walked out. I was watching from the stairs and I saw his face. I thought it would look angry, but it didn't. Just terribly sad.'

'Did he know you saw him?'

Mark shook his head. 'He'd have hated that. He doesn't like people to know how he feels.'

He fell silent. Then he said unexpectedly, 'I keep wishing I could help him.'

She gave him a quick look of surprise, asking, 'Shouldn't he be helping you?'

'We help each other. Well, that's what I wish. I want to be—it's just that—if only—'

His shoulders sagged and she saw the glint of tears on his cheeks. Evie abandoned words and took him in her arms, holding him while his shoulders shook.

'I'm sorry,' he sobbed.

'You've nothing to be sorry about. If you're sad you need to cry, and tell someone.'

'There isn't anyone,' he sobbed. 'Nobody understands.'

She did the only thing she could—tightened her arms and rocked back and forth, trying to comfort him.

A sound made her look up to see Justin standing in the open door. He stood dead still as though amazement had stopped him in his tracks, and she was reminded of the way he had looked at her on the terrace.

Quietly she shook her head, and he retreated without a word.

Mark seemed unaware. He freed himself and straightened up, wiping his eyes and managing a smile.

'Sorry,' he said again.

'Don't be,' she told him.

He was obviously embarrassed, as though feeling he'd given way to an unmanly display.

Sweet heaven! she thought. He's only twelve years old.

'It's getting late,' she said. 'Why don't you go to bed?'

'Will you come and say goodnight before you go?'

'Yes, I promise.'

She gave him another hug, then went downstairs, feeling thoughtful.

Through the open door of the front room she could see Justin, and walked in.

'Is he all right?' Justin asked gruffly.

'Not really. But he's calmed down, and he's going to bed. I promised to look in and say goodnight before I leave, but I think you should go up to him now.'

'There's no point,' he said wearily. 'This has happened before. He won't talk to me. He hates me.'

'He doesn't,' she said at once.

He looked at her sharply. 'You know that? What did he say?'

'I can't tell you what he said. It's confidential between him and me—'

'That's nonsense,' he said impatiently. 'I'm his father—'

'And I'm the person you had to bring in to help you. I'm the one he talks to, although he said very little even to me. I'll tell you that he doesn't hate you. Far from it. But I won't break his confidence. Please understand that that is final.'

'Like hell it is!'

'OK, throw me out!'

'Don't tempt me.'

For answer she pulled out her cellphone and dialled. 'Andrew?'

Justin's hand closed over hers, gripping her so tightly that it hurt. 'It's better if you stay.'

'Really?' she said, freeing her hand and flexing the fingers. 'I'm glad you made your mind up about that. I can't stand a man who dithers.'

He drew a deep breath. 'Now Andrew will be wondering what happened. You'd better call him back.'

'No need. I wasn't really connected.'

'Playing games?'

'No, just warning you not to try to push me around. I'll help all I can, for the sake of that poor child. But it has to be on my terms, because they're the only ones I can use.'

'I'm the same way myself,' he said grimly.

'Then one of us is going to have to give in.'

She realised then how far she had travelled in a short time. Once she'd feared to antagonise Justin in case it rebounded on Mark. But now her instincts were telling her that he only respected people who stood up to him.

Deference equalled disaster.

Besides, she didn't do deference. She didn't know how.

From the thunderous silence she guessed he was assessing his options, realising that they were limited, but not knowing how to admit the fact.

'Don't you think you should tell me what's really happening?' she said. 'Why did Mark go to that cemetery? You said his mother was dead, so I thought she must be buried there, but he says not.'

'No, she's not. Did he say anything else? Or can't you tell me?'

'He said she ought to be there.'

'Hell!' he said softly.

'What did he mean?'

'My wife left us two years ago.'

'Us?'

'She left us both. There was another man. She went to live with him in Switzerland.'

'She didn't take her son with her?' Evie asked, aghast. 'Or did you stop her?'

'I wouldn't have stopped her if she'd wanted him, but I don't think she even thought of it,' he said in a soft voice that had a hint of savagery.

Evie rubbed her hand over her eyes.

'I just don't understand how any mother can do that,' she said distractedly. 'To leave a man—well, it happens if the relationship isn't working. But to abandon a defenceless child—'

'It's the crime of crimes,' Justin said sombrely. 'It's unnatural, unforgivable—'

He stopped. Evie stared at him, alerted by something in his voice that went beyond anger. Hatred.

'That poor kid,' Evie breathed. 'Did she stay in touch?'

'She wrote to him, telephoned sometimes. There were presents at Christmas and birthdays. But he wasn't invited to visit her. The new boyfriend didn't want him, you see, and he was much more important to her than her son.'

Again there was that bitter edge of something that was more than anger. More like pain.

'It must have devastated him,' she murmured. 'How does he cope?'

'He's brave and strong,' Justin said unexpectedly. 'And he knows what the world is like now.'

'He's too young to learn that side of the world,' Evie said quickly.

He gave a mirthless laugh.

'Is there a proper age for a boy to learn that his mother doesn't want him?'

'No, of course not,' she agreed.

'Any age is too young, but it happens when it happens, ten, nine—seven.'

As he said 'seven' his voice changed, making her look at him. But he didn't seem to notice her. He was talking almost to himself.

'And then the whole world becomes unreal, because it can't have happened, yet it has happened. All the reference points are gone and there's only chaos. Disbelief becomes a refuge when there's nothing else.'

'Yes,' she agreed. 'That's how it must be.'

'But it isn't a reliable refuge,' he said in a low voice. 'The world blows it apart again and again, and it becomes harder to find excuses to believe the thing that's least painful.'

'Mr Dane—what are you telling me?'

'I'd have done anything to save my son from the knowledge that his mother rejected him. I stalled on the divorce, went out to Switzerland to see her, begged her to return to us. I hated her by then but I'd have taken her back for his sake.

'I even bought this house for her. It's bigger, better than the one we had. She liked nice things. I thought—'

'You thought you could get her back by spending money?' Evie said, speaking cautiously.

'She wouldn't even come home for a while, even to look at it. She was besotted by her lover. She cared about nothing else.'

'What happened?'

'She died. They died together when his car crashed. I was over there at the time, and since she was still legally my wife it fell to me to oversee her funeral. I suppose it should have occurred to me to bring her home, but it didn't. She's buried in Switzerland.'

'But—Mark—you were willing to do so much to get her back for him—'

'When she was alive, yes. But when she was dead, what difference could it make?'

She stared at him, nonplussed by a man who could be so sensitively generous on the one hand, and so dully oblivious on the other.

'I think it would have made a difference to Mark to have her nearby, even if she was dead,' she tried to explain. 'People need a focus for their grief, somewhere where they can feel closer to the person they've lost. That's what graves are really for.

'And Mark feels it more because you sold the house where she used to be and made him live in a place where she never was. So he can't go around and remember that this was where they shared a joke, and that was where she used to make his tea.

'He needs those memories, but where does he go for

them now? This great mausoleum, which is empty when he comes home every day?'

'Not empty. Lily's here, and he wouldn't want me. You seem to see everything, surely you've seen that?'

'I've seen that the two of you aren't as close as you ought to be. There has to be something you can do about that. I'm guessing you don't spend very much time with him.'

'I have to work all hours. The business doesn't run itself. I created it and I need to keep my eye on it all the time.'

'And it's more important than your son?'

'I do the best I can for my son,' he snapped.

'Then your best is lousy.'

'I'm trying to make a good life for him—'

'Yes, I've seen that ''good life'' upstairs. The latest computer, the latest printer, the latest digital camera—'

'All right, you think I put too much emphasis on money,' he broke in, 'but you can rely on money. It doesn't betray you. And what you've bought really belongs to you.'

'So then you control it?'

'Right,' he agreed, not seeing the trap she'd opened up at his feet.

'And that's what really matters, isn't it?' she challenged him. 'Control.'

'Sometimes it's important to be in control of things. In fact, it's always important.'

'Just things? Or people. Why did your wife *really* leave you?'

He flashed her a look of pure hatred. 'I guess I didn't pay enough,' he snapped.

Before she could answer he walked out of the room and slammed the door.

Evie was left silently cursing herself.

I had no right to say that about his wife. She sighed. *Why do I keep losing my temper? Now I'll have to find him and apologise. Oh, hell! Why don't I grow up?*

Hearing him outside the door, she braced herself for the worst, but his manner, when he entered, was quieter.

'Shall we start again?' he asked mildly.

'That would be a good idea. Please forget that last question. I had no right—'

'It's over,' he said hastily. 'Besides, all the worst you think of me is probably true, and you'd be the first person to say so if you hadn't decided it was wiser to be tactful.'

She let out a long breath at his insight. *'Touché,'* she said at last.

He gave her an ironic look. 'It's good for my pride if I win the odd point or two.'

'I don't think the worst of you,' she said. 'I think you're just floundering.'

'That's true. I don't know what to say to Mark, what to do for him. We don't speak the same language. What you say about moving house may be right, but I meant it for the best.'

'I wish I could help—' she sighed '—but I'm not even going to be here much longer. I leave when term's over. But I'll stay in touch with Mark, if you like, from anywhere in the world.'

'I'd appreciate that.'

'Now I'll go up and see him, because I promised.'

'Thank you. Then I'll take you home.'

'There's no need. I can call a cab.'

'Miss Wharton, I will take you home,' he said firmly. He came upstairs with her and they stopped outside

Mark's door. Evie raised her hand to knock, then thought better of it and opened the door a crack.

'I'm awake,' came Mark's voice at once.

Laughing, she slipped inside and went to sit on the bed, giving him a hug.

'I'm going now,' she said. 'I just came to say goodnight. And thank you for the pictures. I'll give you back the memory stick at school.'

'You will be there?'

'For a bit longer.' She kissed his cheek. 'Bye!'

He flung his arms about her neck. 'Bye!'

Then he saw his father standing in the doorway and removed his arms.

'Hallo, Dad,' he said politely.

'I'm going to drive Miss Wharton home, son.'

'Goodnight.'

If only he would smile at his father, Evie thought. Or at least stop being so woodenly polite. But Mark didn't say another word as she and Justin left the room.

Downstairs, Justin stopped for a word with Lily before leading Evie out to his car.

'Where to?'

She gave him her address and he swung out on to the road. As he drove he said, 'I'm sorry about your ruined evening with your boyfriend.'

'I'll call him when I get in.'

'What will you tell him?'

'The truth. What else?'

'Might he not misunderstand?'

'He won't, as long as I stick to the facts.'

'Are you one of those terrifyingly honest people who always tell the truth about everything?'

She laughed. 'No, I'm not as bad as that. And honesty really has nothing to do with it. It's just that lies have a habit of backfiring on you. I learned that when I was ten.'

In the darkness of the car she just sensed him grinning.

'I learned a lot earlier than that,' he said.

'I even think that honesty can sometimes be an over-rated virtue.'

'Heresy!'

'No, just that sometimes you have to choose between honesty and kindness, and kindness is usually better. My home is just up ahead, in that apartment block.'

'How do you manage with the motorbike?'

'I park it in the basement garage. If you drop me on the kerb here—'

'Actually, I was hoping to come in and talk to you for a while.'

Before she could answer her mobile phone rang.

'I guess that's Andrew,' Justin said. 'You might still save your evening with him. OK, I'll drop you here. Goodnight.'

It wasn't the moment she would have chosen for Andrew to call, but she had no choice but to get out of the car. Justin closed the door behind her and sped away into the darkness, leaving her to answer the phone call, which turned out to be a wrong number.

Evie looked for Mark at school on the following Monday, but there was no sign of him, and Debra said that his father had called to say he had a cold and would be off for a few days.

She'd brought the memory stick in to return to him, but now she wrote him a little note saying that the pictures were lovely, and including her email address and sent the whole thing off in a package.

The following evening his reply was waiting on her computer, with some attached pictures of the puppies. She thanked him, and they settled into an amiable gossip that lasted for the next few days until she wrote at last:

> *If I don't see you before I go, I promise to email you from all over the place. I'm off to my seaside cottage now. I'll send you some pics of it, taken with my digital camera. If you can work yours I'm sure I can learn to work mine.*

She had briefly considered calling at the house to see him, but decided against it. She was leaving soon, and it wasn't kind to encourage Mark to cling to her.

She wondered if Justin would ask her to visit the child, but there was no word from him. Obviously he reckoned that she had outlived her usefulness.

Grumpy but curious, she looked him up on the Internet and what she found there confirmed what Lily had said. Justin Dane took over—people, firms, the world. Starting with nothing fifteen years earlier, he had created an empire out of hard work, genius and ruthlessness.

Before that fifteen years there were gaps in the information. Reading between the lines, all carefully worded to avoid the libel laws, Evie picked up an impression of a wild man, coldly indifferent to the feelings of others, who might even have done a spell in jail.

'A nasty piece of work,' she mused. 'Perhaps it's just as well I won't come into contact with him again.'

CHAPTER FOUR

ON THE last day of term the pupils were due to leave immediately after lunch. Evie skipped lunch and prepared to go quickly. She had a long journey ahead.

'Making your escape?' Debra said, looking in while she was clearing up her things.

'It's not exactly an escape.'

'That's all you know. The Head is talking about kidnapping you and locking you up in a cupboard until next term.'

Evie laughed. 'Then I'd better make a run for it.'

'Is this from the kids?' Debra indicated a large card with many signatures scrawled on it.

'Yes, isn't it sweet of them?'

'I don't see Mark's name. He didn't manage to get back in time then?'

'No, and I'm sorry not to have the chance to say goodbye to him. On the other hand, he might have come to rely on me too much, so maybe it's best as it is. I just wish I didn't have this niggly feeling that I've let him down.'

'You haven't. You did all you could. Now, forget about this place and have a great summer. Are you going anywhere nice?'

'A little seaside cottage for a few weeks.'

'Lovely. With Andrew?'

'He'll join me in a day or two, but it's a bit iffy at the moment. He's very fed up with me and I don't blame him.'

'Never mind. Once you've got him down there you'll bring him round—moonlight on the sea, romantic atmosphere. He won't stand a chance.'

'I hope not.'

Now that she was on the verge of losing Andrew, Evie found herself remembering how sweet-tempered and kind he was, and what a fool she would be to let him go. But all would be well. He would join her, they would spend quality time together, and all their troubles would be forgotten.

What she hadn't told Debra was that she was clearing her things out of the cottage for the last time. It had belonged to an elderly great-uncle, who had recently died and left it to her. But he had also left a mountain of debts and the cottage had to be sold to pay them.

It was time to remove the possessions she'd left there over the years, and she had rented a van to take them. When she'd finished her goodbyes, she went out to where it was parked in the school yard.

It was a relief to head out of noisy, crowded London and south to Cornwall, and Penzance. The sun shone, the countryside soon enveloped her, and her spirits rose.

She had a three hundred mile trip and it was late at night as the van bumped and shuddered down the track to the place where the cottage stood close to the sea.

It was an old-fashioned building, the ground floor taken up by one large room. At one end was a tiny kitchen and at the other end a staircase rose directly to the upper floor.

Her body ached from sitting in one position for so long, and she walked up and down, stretching and rotating her shoulders until she felt human again. After preparing a quick snack she decided to go to bed at once.

The house was a little chilly and would be more cheerful in the morning.

Or perhaps it would be more cheerful when Andrew arrived. Of course he was coming, she assured herself. He'd left a question mark over his arrival, but that was because he was annoyed about her cavalier treatment. It couldn't end like this, and if it did it was Justin Dane's fault for making her stand him up.

Her mind resisted the idea that it was Mark's fault. That vulnerable boy carried enough burdens already without her piling more on him. Perhaps she'd already done so, by leaving without a proper goodbye. She wasn't sure what else she could have done, but the thought troubled her.

She thought about the way she'd fought with Justin. She hadn't meant to fight him, but there didn't seem any other way to communicate with this man. At least he listened while she was insulting him, even if only out of surprise.

If he'd had any decency he'd have come to the school and invited her home to say goodbye to Mark. But it clearly hadn't occurred to him to consider his son's feelings.

She must have been lonelier for Andrew than she realised, because she was suddenly swept by despondency. It would be better in the morning, she promised herself. On that thought she fell asleep.

Next day she went into the village and bought groceries. On her return she started spring-cleaning so that the cottage should be at its best for potential buyers. By keeping busy she could ignore the fact that the telephone didn't ring and there was no sign of Andrew.

She made sandwiches and ate them sitting outside,

watching the sunset again, feeling suddenly very much alone.

But then she heard it. The sound of a car horn followed by crunching as wheels came down the gravel track.

Andrew! she thought, delighted.

She was surprised too, because it was not his way to arrive without calling first, but obviously his feelings had carried him away. In a moment she'd jumped up and raced around the cottage to where a car had just drawn up. Then she saw that the driver was not Andrew.

'You!' she cried, aghast, as Justin Dane climbed out. 'What on earth—?'

Her voice faded as she saw Mark emerging too, smiling when he saw her. She smiled back and made her voice sound pleased as she greeted him.

'We were in the area and thought we'd look you up,' Justin said.

'You just happened to be in this remote part of the world?' She couldn't keep the scepticism out of her voice.

'Well—it's a little more complicated than that,' he said, sounding as though he were choosing his words carefully.

'Let's go inside and you can tell me how complicated it is,' she said, trying to sound agreeable, although inwardly she was cross.

Once before he'd spoiled things for her and Andrew. Now he was going to do it again.

Mark darted away around the side of the house, calling, 'Hey, look how close we are to the sea!'

'I know what you're thinking,' Justin said.

'I wonder if you do,' she mused wryly.

'I shouldn't have just come here without warning, I know.'

'Mark has my email address. You could have used it.'

'But you might have said no.'

She threw up her hands in despair.

'In that case, you were probably right not to take the risk,' she said with ironic appreciation of his methods.

'I did it for Mark. He was upset at not seeing you again. We came to the school yesterday; you'd already gone. In fact, I'm in Mark's bad books because he wanted to go sooner and I promised to get home early from work, but I got held up and then—'

'So it was your fault that you missed me,' she said, amused despite herself.

'Yes, and then the caretaker told me you'd left in a van, but didn't know where.'

'Otherwise you'd have come chasing after me like we were in some Grand Prix.'

'Mark was upset. And may I remind you who it was told me that I should listen more to him?'

'Oh, very clever!' But what could she say? It was true. 'So how did you know how to find me?'

'You told Mark you had a cottage by the sea.'

'I didn't tell him where.'

'Well, I just—' reading wrath in her eyes again he became deliberately vague '—I just asked around.'

'Where?' she asked implacably.

'I went to your flat. One of the neighbours was very helpful—'

'You mean you had me investigated like a criminal?'

'I had to find out where you were.'

They glared, each baffled to find the other so unreasonable. Justin wondered why she couldn't understand that he'd done whatever was necessary to get what he wanted. That was what he always did, and it seemed simple enough to him.

To Evie it was also simple. She disliked being treated like prey to be hunted down for his convenience. But she wouldn't say so while Mark might be within earshot. The real quarrel could wait until later.

'Dad,' Mark called, reappearing around the side of the building. 'It's a wonderful place. Is it really yours?' This was to Evie.

'Sort of,' she said. 'Come in and have something to eat.'

But Justin said, 'It's getting late. Mark's tired and needs to go to bed soon, so I guess we'll find a hotel, if you'll tell us where the nearest one is.'

It was a direct challenge, and thoroughly unscrupulous.

'You know I won't turn you out at this hour,' she said.

He gave her a smile that was suddenly charming.

'But you can't just put us up without warning. I don't suppose you have the room, and I don't want to inconvenience you—'

'That is not true,' she said, speaking lightly but with a glitter in her eyes that gave him fair warning. 'You do not care if you inconvenience me. You don't care about anything as long as you get your own way. Now shut up and get in there before I stamp hard on your feet.'

The smile changed into a grin. He'd won again.

Mark was also grinning, Evie was glad to notice. For his sake she forgave his father everything.

Well, almost everything.

From the amount of luggage he hauled into the cottage it was clear that he'd come prepared to stay for a while.

But it would just be until Andrew arrived, and not a moment longer.

'It's not what you're used to,' she warned. 'No luxury. Just basic.'

'You wouldn't be trying to put me off?' he said, regarding her ironically.

'Would I do that?'

Again he gave that grin. This was Justin Dane in holiday mood. The grin was surprisingly attractive with a blazing quality that could lift a woman's spirits unless she was on her guard against him. Which she was.

Mark dashed in and looked around at the large downstairs room with its big open fireplace.

'It's great!' he enthused. 'Just like a picture book.'

'I didn't think modern boys read that sort of picture book,' she said.

'Not now,' he agreed, 'but when I was a kid.' He looked round and found something else to please him. 'No central heating,' he said ecstatically.

'That's a plus?' Justin queried.

'Radiators would have spoiled it,' Mark explained.

'That's what Uncle Joe used to say.' Evie chuckled. 'He said he didn't want to spoil the place with a lot of "new-fangled rubbish". We used to put electric fires on in winter.'

'If there's somewhere to lay our heads,' Justin said, 'that's all we ask.'

'You can have the guest room. It's got two single beds.'

She'd just finished cleaning the room. Now she found linen and dumped it on the beds.

'It won't take you long to make them up,' she said, smiling at Justin. 'Mark, why don't we leave your father to it, while you and I go into the kitchen and we'll see what there is for supper?'

She departed, throwing a challenging look over her shoulder. He regarded her with his eyebrows raised, but did not seem disconcerted.

When they were in the kitchen Evie muttered to Mark, 'What is your father playing at?'

Mark's shrug was eloquent. 'Dad sets his heart on something and he has to have it. He promised me I could talk to you again.'

'Even if it means chasing me halfway across the country *and missing a whole day's work*?'

Mark gave a snort of delighted laughter.

'Actually he won't be missing that much,' he said. 'He's brought his laptop computer. He can send and read emails at any hour. And he's got his mobile phone so that all his calls won't go on to your phone—'

'*All* his calls? How many calls will there be, and how long is he planning to stay?'

'The actual time doesn't matter,' Mark said wisely. 'Dad can get through more business in five minutes than anyone he knows. That's what he says, anyway. And he always calls America in the evening because they're five hours behind us, and he says that's really useful—'

'In other words, he isn't actually planning to take any time off at all. It'll be business as usual, just in a different setting.'

Mark nodded.

'Until I tell him to leave.'

'You wouldn't,' Mark said, awed by this reckless courage.

'I would. I'll be straight with you, Mark. At the right time, I'll square up to your father and order him off my premises.'

'Wow!' he said, impressed. He moved closer and spoke like a conspirator. 'Will you promise me something?'

She too leaned close. 'What?' she whispered dramatically.

'That when you order Dad off your premises I can be there to see. *Promise* me.'

She laughed. 'You wretched boy. All right, I promise you can be there to enjoy it.'

They jumped apart as Justin appeared with air of suppressed triumph.

'Everything is done upstairs,' he said. 'If you'd care to look.'

'Why are you looking so pleased with yourself?' she asked.

'Come and see.'

She was beginning to suspect the truth, but it was still a surprise to find the beds made perfectly and all the clothes neatly hung up in the wardrobe.

She realised that he was watching her closely, enjoying her expression.

'Well done,' she said. 'Can you cook as well?'

'Try me.'

'I intend to,' she said incredulously.

But again he proved himself better than her doubts. His egg and chips might not have been haute cuisine but they were properly cooked, even if both father and son drenched everything in tomato ketchup. She had to smile at the sight of them acting in unison, wiping their plates with bread, fearful of losing the last smidgen of ketchup.

When the meal was over she leaned back, watching him, her arms folded.

'Well?' she said.

'Well?'

She inclined her head slightly towards the sink.

'I did the cooking,' he said indignantly.

'Yeah, but we invited ourselves, Dad,' Mark muttered.

'Fine. I'll wash, you dry.' He rose. 'Where's the washing-up liquid?'

'I'll do it,' she said, laughing.

In the end they all did it together in an atmosphere that was more pleasant than she would have dared to hope. Afterwards Mark asked to watch the television, and was amazed to discover that the set only received four terrestrial channels and had no teletext. Nor was there a video.

'Gosh, it's like history!' he gasped.

'Mark!' Justin said sharply.

'It's all right.' Evie chuckled. 'He didn't mean it rudely. It must be like something out of the Dark Ages to a modern child.'

In the end they settled down to watch the news, until they heard an ominous sound outside. Evie turned down the sound and they all listened in alarm.

'It's raining!' Mark whispered in horror.

They went outside, where it was pelting down.

'It'll be all right in the morning,' Evie said.

Mark looked at her. 'Promise?'

'Promise,' she said recklessly. 'And now I think you should go to bed. It's late and tomorrow's a big day.'

'Can we go swimming?'

'What about your cold?'

'It's better, honestly. Isn't it, Dad?'

'I wouldn't have brought him here otherwise,' Justin assured her. 'Mark, you heard what Miss Wharton said. Up to bed.'

Mark took her hand. 'Miss Wharton—can I call you Evie?'

'Mark!'

'Well, I'm not his teacher any more,' she said. 'Evie it is.'

Mark departed, satisfied.

'I apologise,' Justin groaned.

'Don't. He's just being friendly.'

'How friendly do you think he'll be tomorrow when it rains?'

'It won't rain.'

'How can you be sure?'

'Because I promised him. You heard me.'

'Yes, but—'

'It won't rain. I promised.' She yawned. 'I think I'll go to bed too. Sea air makes me sleepy. 'G'night.'

'Goodnight.'

In her room she undressed and went to bed, listening for the sound of him coming upstairs. She was still listening when she fell asleep.

She didn't know what roused her, but she awoke suddenly in the darkness. The clock by her bed showed two o'clock. She listened and thought she could hear a voice talking in the distance.

Pulling a dressing gown on over her pyjamas, she crept out into the corridor and went to the top of the stairs, from where she could see down into the main room.

Just as Mark had predicted, Justin had set up a laptop computer and was staring at the screen at the same time as talking into his cellphone. He spoke softly, but Evie could pick up the tense note in his voice.

'I'm sorry but I just couldn't take the call this afternoon—I know what I said but I had important business—'

She went quietly downstairs and into the kitchen. By

the time she returned with two large mugs of tea he was off the phone.

'Thanks,' he said, taking one. 'Sorry if I disturbed you, but I had to catch up with my work somehow.'

'Yes, you've obviously come prepared. I'm surprised you could put work aside long enough to drive down here. All those hours not at the computer, not on the phone, not making contacts.'

'I don't bother to make contacts any more. I don't need to. People contact me.'

'You arrogant so-and-so,' she said, amused. 'Anyway, it isn't true. There's always someone bigger you can be doing business with.'

'That's true,' he reflected. 'Why don't you say out-right that you're just surprised that I put Mark first?'

'Well—'

'Don't worry, you've already made your poor opinion of me pretty plain, and I'm not arguing with it.'

'Hey, I didn't exactly—'

'Are you saying you don't have a poor opinion of me?'

'Well, it improved when you took the trouble to drive down here for Mark's sake. Although it takes a dive at your way of moving people around like pieces on your own private chessboard.'

'Do I do that? Well, maybe sometimes.'

'You know quite well that you do.'

'Miss Wharton—' he began in a patient voice, but she stopped him.

'What did you say?'

'Nothing.'

'You did, you called me something.'

'I called you Miss Wharton.'

'But why?'

'I thought it was your name.'

'But why aren't you calling me Evie?'

'Because you haven't given me your permission.'

She tore her hair. 'I gave it to Mark.'

'Yes, to Mark. Not to me.'

He was serious, she realised. Was it possible for a modern man to be so old-fashioned? Against her will she realised that there was something charming about it.

'Why are you smiling?' he asked suspiciously.

'It's nothing.' It wouldn't do to tell him she found him charming. He would hate it. 'Call me Evie. And look, you can stay for a short time, but I'll have to ask you to leave without warning. I'm expecting someone.'

'Andrew?'

'Yes, not that it's any of your business.'

'When's he coming?'

'I'm not sure, but when I know he's on his way you really do have to go. He and I have a lot of ground to make up.'

'You mean because of the other evening?'

'Among other things.'

'But surely you made it up when he called you?'

She made a face. 'That wasn't him. It was someone trying to sell me insurance.'

A tremor passed over his face as he tried to suppress his grin and didn't quite manage it.

'Oh, go on, laugh,' she said. 'The poor man who called me didn't think it was so funny when I'd finished giving him a piece of my mind.'

'Having been on the receiving end of a piece of your mind, he has my sympathy.'

'Well, I apologised to him in the end.'

'Did Andrew ever call you?'

'I called him. Same thing.'

He didn't comment on this, but asked thoughtfully, 'Are you in love with him?'

She drew a sharp breath. 'That is none of your business.'

'I suppose not, but I've asked it now, so why not tell me? Either you love him or you're not sure, and the reason you dump him so easily is because you're actually trying to tell him to get lost.'

Since Andrew himself had said something of the kind she was briefly at a loss for words. She decided that she preferred Justin Dane when she could regard him with outright hostility, simple and uncomplicated.

'Yes, I am in love with Andrew,' she said firmly.

He was silent for a moment. 'I see,' he said at last. 'So you want us to leave tomorrow?'

'I didn't say that.'

'But if he finds me here he might think you're playing around. Yes, I know, you'll tell him the truth, but will he believe you?'

'Of course. We trust each other completely. And he won't turn up without warning, he'll call me first.'

'He might do it differently this time.'

'Not Andrew.'

'Solid and reliable?'

'Yes.'

'Doesn't that make life a bit repetitive?'

She regarded him with smouldering eyes. It was simply unforgivable that he should echo her own thoughts. Her own *previous* thoughts, she corrected hastily, dating from before she'd realised how foolish she would be to lose him.

'I will not discuss Andrew with you,' she said.

'You know, I think that's probably a very wise decision.'

They eyed each other and she realised that her previous impression had been correct. He really could be charming.

'I was very impressed by your domestic skills,' she said. 'All that cooking and bed-making. Your mother did a really good job on you.'

He didn't answer, and when she looked at him she found him staring into the distance.

'Hey, I was just paying a compliment to your mother.'

'No need. I never knew her.'

'You mean she died early?'

'Something like that. I'm going to pack up for the night now.' He began switching off his computer.

'Did I say something wrong?' she asked, puzzled at the way he had suddenly closed a door on her in a manner that was uncannily similar to his son's.

'Not at all.'

'Did I offend you, mentioning your mother?'

'Of course not. There, everything's switched off. By the way, I think it's stopped raining.'

'Of course. What did I tell you?'

He regarded her for a moment, taking in the impish gleam in her eyes, and unable to stop smiling at her.

'Any minute now you'll almost have me believing that you cast a magic spell,' he said.

'Maybe I did. I think I'll just leave you to wonder about that. By the way, what about swimming trunks? I mean, if you weren't expecting to stay—'

'We do have them. I thought I might, just possibly, prevail on you.'

'Hogwash!' she said sternly. 'Has anyone ever managed to turn you away at the door?'

'The last man who tried was fending off my take-over bid.'

'No guesses who won.'

'Well,' he said, considering, 'I took him over, but he made me pay more than I'd meant to.'

She threw up her hands in mock horror. 'Disaster!'

'No, just something you have to be prepared for in business. You have to start out knowing what a thing is worth to you and how high you're prepared to go. Winning at a cost is still winning.'

'At *any* cost?'

'That depends what you're aiming to win. Only a few things are worth any cost.'

'What are you aiming to win now?'

'My son's confidence—his trust—his love—at any cost.'

That surprised and silenced her. She had suspected it, but hearing him say it warned her that she had partly misread him. There was more to him than she had believed. It was becoming possible to like him.

Then he said, 'But I need your help; that's why I'm here. You're vital if I'm to have any chance.'

And suddenly she was a pawn on his chessboard again, irritated into saying, 'So you worked out the cost of working at half-speed for a few days and decided it was affordable. But where do I figure in your equation?'

'I told you—vital.'

'But supposing I come with a heavy cost?' she fenced. She was beginning to find fencing with this man strangely exhilarating.

He raised an eyebrow.

'If you do,' he said with soft irony, 'perhaps you should tell me now, so that I can make the necessary arrangements.'

'Oh, get lost!' she said, cheated of her victory. 'I'm going to bed.'

CHAPTER FIVE

LOOKING out of her window next morning, Evie gave thanks that her reckless promise to Mark had been kept. It was a perfect day; the sun was riding high and making the waves glitter almost blindingly.

Mark was leaning out from the next window, beaming and making ecstatic thumbs up signs. She raised her own thumbs in return, laughing and enjoying his happiness.

Downstairs, she put on the kettle and began preparing breakfast. After a few minutes they both joined her. Evie stared at the sight of Justin in shorts and casual shirt.

She stared even more when he gave her a solemn bow, then glanced at his son, as if asking if he'd done it right. But Mark wasn't satisfied.

'Oh, mighty one!' he cried, bowing low.

'Mark insists that we do this,' Justin explained. 'He says you're magic because you made the rain stop and the sun come out. So we must propitiate you, mighty one.'

To her delight he bowed again.

'All right,' she chuckled. 'That's enough grovelling—for today, anyway. Come and have breakfast.'

'Can't we go to the beach now?' Mark begged.

'Later, when the water's had a chance to warm up a bit,' she told him. 'You've just recovered from a cold.'

'And we should go out and buy some food first,' Justin said.

Going around the local supermarket gave her another glimpse of his many facets. Not only could he cook but he also knew what to buy.

He had good legs too, she thought distractedly.

After filling the trolley Justin stopped by the wine shelves. 'White or red?'

'White, please,' she said.

'Can we go to the beach *now*?' Mark asked plaintively as they drove home. 'It's ever so hot.'

'We could make some sandwiches and take them with us,' Evie said.

They agreed on that, packing up a picnic basket before setting off.

The road from the cottage to the beach was strewn with large rocks that had to be negotiated on foot. At the far end the sand spread out into an area of pure gold, stretching away to the sea. It was a small area, flanked on two sides by more rocks, which made it almost like a private beach.

Other holiday makers had been known to brave the rocks for a while, but the trouble of having to climb back over them to get an ice cream was a deterrent. Today they had the place to themselves.

Evie had changed, putting on her swimsuit beneath her clothes. She was a little troubled by that swimsuit. It was a bikini, chosen with Andrew in mind, and ideally she would not have worn it now. But she hadn't thought of it until too late.

Well, it might be worse, she told herself. *As bikinis go it's fairly modest. Even the top is respectable, and I haven't got much to display anyway. First time I've ever been glad of that.*

They tucked into sandwiches and orange squash, but Mark ate very little.

'You need more than that,' Evie protested.

'Nope,' he said, shaking his head firmly. ''Cos otherwise you'll say I mustn't go swimming after a big meal. So I've only eaten a little meal, and I'm going now.'

Before they could stop him he jumped to his feet and shot away across the sands to plunge into the sea.

'Let's go,' Justin said, pulling off his clothes and haring after his son.

Now there was no time to worry about revealing too much. Evie tore off her own clothes and sped after them, rejoicing in the wind whipping past her, the sun on her bare skin, and then the glorious moment of diving in.

She came up, looking around, then saw the two of them preparing to scoop up water and douse her with spray. She screamed and backed away, trying to fend them off. But they splashed her without mercy until she had to sink right under the surface to escape them.

'I give in, I give in,' she cried at last as they roared with laughter.

They splashed around together for a while, with Evie keeping in the background so that father and son could be together. At last Mark declared he was hungry.

'Come and finish your lunch,' Evie said.

'OK.'

'I'll have a longer swim first,' Justin said, and turned to head out to sea.

Back at base Evie and Mark dried themselves off and settled down on large towels.

'I'm ever so glad we came,' Mark confided. 'So's Dad.'

'Did he tell you that?'

He shook his head, spraying crumbs.

'Dad doesn't say things like that,' he said, when he

could speak again. 'But he's cheerful. 'Spect it's 'cos of you.'

'No, it's 'cos of you,' she said. 'He likes being with you. But I'm glad he's cheerful. He's much nicer to be around when you can get a smile out of him.'

'Yes,' Mark said with feeling.

She looked out to sea. 'Where's he gone?'

Mark produced binoculars from his bag. 'There,' he said, handing them to her. 'He's a long way out.'

After a moment she saw Justin's dark head and the movements of his muscular arms, pounding through the waves. As she watched, he turned back towards the rocks where they stretched out into the sea. Reaching them, he hauled himself up and stood for a moment, his wet body gleaming in the sun. Then he dived back in, swam in a wide circle and climbed back on to the rocks.

He stood there long enough for Evie to study him and realise how conventional clothes failed to do him justice. She had known that he was tall, broad-shouldered and long-limbed, but, seeing him almost naked, she suddenly understood many things. His air of walking through the world like a prince was not based on his wealth, but on the proud angle at which he carried his head.

There was the shape of his body, lean and taut, not an ounce of fat, despite his muscular build. He might have been an athlete, or a man doing heavy manual labour. But a silk-suited tycoon flying the world and making deals—that wouldn't have occurred to her.

'Evie!' Mark touched her arm.

With a start she came back to reality, lowering the binoculars.

'Sorry—what?'

'I kept calling and calling you, and you didn't hear.'

'I got distracted by the scenery,' she said vaguely.

'I've poured you some more orange juice.'

She tried to concentrate on the snack, but the sun had dazzled her and she couldn't blot it out, even with her eyes closed. He was there behind her eyelids, diving in and out of the glare, his body shining in the spray.

When she opened her eyes again she saw him walking up the beach.

'That's better,' he said, dropping down beside them. 'I've been too long without exercise.'

'Somehow I pictured you working out in the gym,' she said.

'In theory I do, but the work piles up and it's always tomorrow.'

'Domani, domani, sempre domani!' she declaimed, with a knowing look at Mark.

Justin stared from one to the other.

'Tomorrow, tomorrow, always tomorrow,' Mark translated.

'There, I told you he was one of my best pupils,' Evie said triumphantly.

Mark got to his feet. 'I'm going to explore.'

'Don't go too far,' Justin said quickly.

'Promise.' Mark sped off before he could be asked for any further promises.

'I've never seen him have such a good time,' Justin said, watching the slight figure scampering away. 'Thank you.'

'Didn't you two ever go on seaside holidays before?'

'We went away while his mother was alive, but it was always somewhere like Disneyland. That's what kids seem to want these days, but this—' He made a gesture indicating their surroundings. 'He's happy.'

'Did your family ever take you to the seaside when you were a child?'

She wondered if he had heard her, because he stared straight ahead without answering. At last she realised that he had simply blanked out the question.

If she knew the reason for that, she mused, she might understand more about Mark's inner turmoil.

'Whatever is he doing now?' Justin asked, his eyes on his son.

They could see Mark on the rocks, staring down into a pool, evidently fascinated by something he saw there.

'It's probably a crab, or a starfish,' Evie said. 'I used to look at them in that same pool when I was a kid.'

'Did your family own this place?'

'My Great-Uncle Joe. He was a wonderful old boy, and he virtually brought me up after my parents died, when I was twelve. But it was more than giving me a home. I loved my parents, but they were very conventional people. They reckoned there was only one right way to do everything. It was stifling.

'Joe was just the opposite. He thought there was no right way to do anything, you just had to choose the wrong one that suited you. His motto was "To blazes with the lot of 'em!"'

He grinned and rolled over on his back, propping himself up on one elbow to look up at her.

'I'll bet a twelve-year-old loved it.'

'It was great,' she said, sighing in happy remembrance, 'like having a light come on in the world. Joe reckoned the only crime was to do what other people expected. And he thought it was a virtue to offend at least one person every day.'

'Oh, that's where you—'

'No, I never quite went that far,' she told him repressively.

'Just me, huh?' he asked with a raised eyebrow.

'Just people who deserve it. Shall I continue?'

'Please do.'

'I was really sad when I had to leave here to go to college. I even thought of not going, but Joe lost his temper and nearly threw me out. He said if I didn't seize my chance, I needn't show my face here again. So I went, but I always came back in summer. To me it was the most wonderful place in the world.'

She sighed happily, looking around her at the beauty. But then her face grew sad.

'He died recently and left it to me, but then I found he had huge debts. I'd had no idea. I used to send him money to help out, but apparently it all went into betting shops.

'I never knew about his problem, and I have a horrid feeling it only developed after I left, because he was lonely. Now the cottage has to be sold to pay the debts. I'm just here to clear out my stuff and take a last look.'

'You're going to lose this place?' he asked, sitting up and speaking sharply.

'Just as soon as there's a decent offer. I thought of trying to keep it by paying off the debts—I just can't afford it. I even thought—'

She was interrupted by the sound of her cellphone. Justin didn't miss her sudden alertness, or the eager way she scrabbled in her bag for the phone. He saw the sudden sagging of her shoulders as she said, 'Oh, hi, Sally.'

There followed a conversation about proofs, galleys and corrections, and it was no surprise when she hung up and said, 'That was my editor, about a book I have coming out next month.'

'Not Andrew, then? Has he called you at all?'

'I've only been here two days.'

'And in those two days,' Justin said relentlessly, 'has he called you?'

'Please don't interrogate me, Mr Dane.'

'I'll take that as a no. If I were in love with a woman I wouldn't forget to call her.'

'Well, maybe he doesn't want to seem too anxious. We've been having a few problems. That's why he's coming here.'

'But *is* he coming here?'

She ignored this. 'We'll spend some time together sorting things out.'

'It's a bit early in the relationship for that, isn't it?'

'I don't know what you mean,' she said, wishing he'd drop the subject. But he wouldn't, almost as if he knew how uneasy it made her.

'Sorting things out is what happens when people have been together a while,' he said, 'and things have turned sour, but they want to recapture the magic. If you're "sorting out" in the courtship stage, he's the wrong guy.'

'I'll decide about that, thank you.'

'You can decide what you like, but he's the wrong guy. Why pick on him? Unless you're afraid of being an old maid.'

'Get lost!' she said amiably.

'Well, it has to be said. You're no spring chicken. You must be pushing—what? Forty?'

'Thirty!'

He roared with laughter. 'I had a bet with myself that you'd tell me your age by the end of the day.'

She made a face at him and he laughed again. 'So, thirty, and he's your last chance. Life has passed you by. Men have passed you by. You're pretty enough in a dim light, but nobody's offered you lifetime commitment.'

His eyes were wicked and she smiled back, disconcerted by the sudden reappearance of his charm.

'So, my guess is that you put up with any amount of awkward behaviour on his part, for fear of losing him.'

'No way,' she said. 'It's my awkward behaviour that's caused the problems.'

'Just because you stood him up that night, he's throwing a wobbly?'

'Don't you throw a wobbly if you get stood up?'

'I don't get stood up,' he said with an assurance that was so complete she almost admired it.

'You are the most arrogant, conceited man I've ever met.'

'I'm just recording facts. He can't take it that you put him second that night.'

'It's not the only time—other things happen, and get in the way. But that's over now.'

'Because he's your hero? The one and only whose voice makes your heart beat? The man who—?'

'All right!' she said, trying not to laugh. 'It's a bit more prosaic than that, but, like you said, old age is creeping up on me.'

'Yeah, sure,' he said in a tone of disbelief. Added to the way he looked her figure up and down, it amounted to a definite compliment.

It was the first time he'd even hinted that he admired her as a woman, and it threw her off balance. Suddenly the 'modest' bikini wasn't modest any more. Her bosom was more generous than she'd realised, and the bra was cut low enough to display the fact.

It was like discovering that she'd been naked under his gaze all the time, and had never known it. She could feel herself beginning to blush.

But, just in time, she saw what he was really up to.

He wanted her to think only of Mark, and if that meant fighting off other interests, then he'd do just that.

Well, forewarned was forearmed she thought, amused. It wouldn't hurt to torment him a little.

'The truth is that I'm at a crossroads in my life.' She sighed. 'Freedom's all very well up to a point, but sooner or later a woman wants to settle down with a good man. And then there's security. When I've paid off Joe's debts there won't be much left and I should be looking to the future.'

'You mean you'd marry him for money?'

'Not just that. You said it yourself, he's my hero. His voice makes my heart beat with anticipation—'

She stopped. He was looking at her.

'Well, something like that, anyway.' She laughed.

'You're playing a very cool game. Why aren't you in London, knocking on his door, making sure of him?'

'Because that would send him running in the opposite direction. How would you feel about a woman who threw herself at you? Silly me, I suppose they already do.'

He regarded her satirically. 'Think so?'

'With your money?' she asked airily. 'Of course they do.'

It was a gross slander, she thought, looking at him stretched out on the sand in negligent ease. She had seen him from a distance, but close up he was even more impressive.

She considered this matter entirely dispassionately. Her own preference was for a man like Andrew, built on less spectacular lines, but with a mind that met hers.

And a man's mind was important, she mused. Andrew was intelligent, literary, with fine, sensitive fibres. Justin Dane was undoubtedly intelligent. Or rather, where his own interests were concerned he was shrewd and cunning. He certainly wasn't literary, and she suspected that his fibres resembled thick canvas.

It was just annoying that he had a body designed to send an easily provoked female into a frenzy. Luckily for her, she wasn't easily provoked.

Mark came running up the beach with a little crab which he displayed proudly.

'Look what I've got.'

'Very nice,' Justin said, regarding the object askance.

'Isn't he beautiful?' Evie said, taking the little crab in her hand. 'I used to look for these on this beach when I was a child.'

'What did you do with them?' Mark wanted to know.

'I used to look for someone whose shirt I could drop it down.'

'Really!' Justin said in a voice heavy with significance. 'Let me advise both of you to forget any such idea.'

Then Mark delighted her by asking, 'Not scared, are you, Dad?'

And Justin pleased her even more by grinning and saying, 'Terrified. So remember that, and beware!'

They all laughed. It was the happiest and most relaxed moment that the three of them had shared.

Her phone rang again. Her heart leapt at the thought that it might be Andrew, yet she knew a brief flash of regret that the moment was over.

But it wasn't Andrew. An unfamiliar female voice asked if that was Miss Wharton, then went on to explain that a couple would like to look over the cottage.

'This afternoon, if possible.'

'Yes—yes, of course,' Evie said. 'Do you need directions?'

As she described the way, Justin began to pack up their things, quietly explaining to Mark what was happening. When Evie hung up they were ready to go.

'That was the estate agent,' she said. 'A Mr and Mrs Nicholson will be here to view the cottage in a couple of hours.'

Then she turned away quickly so that her face shouldn't betray how wretched she suddenly felt.

'I suppose a potential buyer is good news,' Justin mused.

'Yes,' she said, trying to convince herself. 'I should go and tidy up.'

They had all left early that morning, not stopping to make beds and do washing-up, in their eagerness to get to the beach. Now they helped her, going around the cottage at speed, shoving things into drawers and hurrying dusters over every spare surface.

The Nicholsons arrived half an hour early and walked in as though they already owned the place. They were rich, middle-aged and insensitive.

'Isn't this just wonderful?' Mrs Nicholson demanded of her husband, standing in the middle of the downstairs room. 'Look at those flagstones. How romantic! And a real open fire! How beautiful! Of course, it'll have to come out.'

'But why, if it's beautiful?' Evie couldn't help asking.

'Unhygienic. All that smoke.'

'It goes up the chimney,' Justin observed.

'But it's still unhygienic,' Mrs Nicholson said firmly. She was plainly a woman who grabbed an idea and hung on to it.

She and her mostly silent husband went through the whole cottage like that, criticising while pronouncing everything beautiful, wonderful, magnificent.

Justin's brow was getting darker, as though this behaviour upset him too, and at last he came up behind
Evie, putting his warm hands firmly on her shoulders
and murmuring into her ear, 'It's perfect, but it's all got
to be changed. To hell with them!'

She growled agreement. His hands vanished from her
shoulders, leaving behind a warm imprint that stayed
with her for several minutes.

'We just love it,' Mrs Nicholson proclaimed at last.
Mr Nicholson nodded without speaking.

'Of course, it's very over-priced,' she charged on.
'We'd expect you to come down.'

'I'm afraid that's not possible.'

For a moment Evie wondered who had spoken. All
she knew for certain was that it wasn't herself. Then she
saw Justin's face. He was giving Mrs Nicholson the kind
of resolute look that she imagined he'd used to close
profitable deals in the past. Evie stared at him, past
speech.

'You see,' he went on, 'Miss Wharton can't make any
agreement. You have to deal with her uncle's executor,
who is obliged, by law, to get the best possible deal. So
I'm afraid he won't be in favour of an ''agreement''—'

'But I'm sure you realise—'

'And I'm sure that you realise that he would be very
displeased with her if she agreed a lower price with you.'

'But surely a private arrangement first—'

'Miss Wharton will give you the executor's number,
and he'll expect your call.'

Sulkily the woman took the number and made a grand
exit, her husband trailing meekly in her wake. Through
the window, the three of them watched the couple get
into a car whose size and luxury left no doubt of their
ability to meet the price.

Evie turned awed eyes on Justin, and found him regarding her with less than his usual confidence.

'Did I go too far?' he asked.

'No,' she said. 'You were terrific. But how——?'

'She was trying to steamroller you and I wasn't going to let it happen. I'm an old hand in the art of not getting steamrollered.'

'I'll bet you are. Thank you.' Then she sighed. 'But I'll have to sell in the end.'

'Yes, but you've got a little more time.'

'Don't you want to sell?' Mark asked her. He'd been listening intently.

She could only shake her head.

The call from the lawyer came an hour later. The Nicholsons had made an offer, but it was below the market price.

'I've refused and we're playing a waiting game,' he said. 'I think they'll go higher if we wait. Or do you think I should make the deal now?'

'No,' she said quickly. 'We should wait.'

'What happened?' Justin asked as soon as she hung up.

'They've made an offer below the price. I'm not taking it.'

'Good for you.'

'Does that mean we can stay here?' Mark asked eagerly.

'Yes, we don't have to go for a bit,' she told him, smiling.

'Yippee!' he crowed. 'We're going to have a wonderful time.'

She hugged him. 'That's right. We're going to have a wonderful time.'

CHAPTER SIX

EVIE had expected Mark to grow quickly bored with an old-fashioned seaside holiday, but it didn't happen. He was eager for even the simplest experiences, and she could almost imagine that she saw herself again in him.

For the next few days they all enjoyed themselves so much that she nearly forgot about her problems. Nobody else came to view the place, and she was able to relish her temporary reprieve.

They went exploring, and Mark listened, entranced, to the tales of pirates. When they actually found a pirate museum he was in seventh heaven. Evie bought him a book called *Black Simeon's Revenge*, which he read in the car all the way home. After supper he fell asleep over it.

The next day Justin found a fisherman with a boat big enough for them all, and they went out to sea. After a day in the salty air they were all sleepy, and Mark actually made the journey back fast asleep with a smile on his face.

Evie watched all this with delight, but she was also puzzled by Justin. He was pleasant, and on the surface all was well between him and his son. But sometimes she happened to glance at him when he thought nobody was looking, and then his smile would be replaced by a look that was distant, almost haggard.

Mark had spoken of a darkness inside his father, and Evie began to sense an air of unreality. Justin was doing his best, but he was following rules that he didn't understand.

Once or twice he came close to losing his temper—about nothing, as far as she could see. He controlled himself quickly and apologised, but she was disturbed, by how trivial were the things that triggered his outbursts. He was living on his nerves, and the strain was pulling him apart. She often caught him watching her with Mark, as though desperately trying to discover something.

Then she told herself that she was being fanciful. He worked long hours at night to keep up with his business, and he was simply very tired. When she found Mark asleep over his book, Justin was also fighting not to nod off.

'Go to bed,' she told him, laughing and yawning.

She was about to say that she too fancied an early night, when the cottage telephone rang.

The other two watched her pick up the receiver and announce herself cheerfully. Then they saw the smile fade from her face. After that she said very little before hanging up and turning to face them.

'That was Uncle Joe's executor,' she said. 'The Nicholsons have upped their offer, and he's accepted it. They want to push the deal through fast, so that they can take possession as soon as possible.'

Dawn was just beginning to glow across the sea when Justin came quietly downstairs, meaning to slip out for an early swim. He was dressed in shorts and his shirt was open, for the day was already growing warm.

He headed for the door, eager to get outside and plunge into the water, but then he stopped, realising that he was not alone.

The figure on the couch was so still and silent that at first he hadn't seen her. Now he moved closer, uncertain what to do next. He supposed he ought to leave and not invade her privacy. Instead he dropped to his knees beside her.

She looked as though she'd been crying, but that might have been a trick of the poor light. Last night she'd been near to tears, following the phone call, but she had brightened up at once, insisting that everything was fine.

But it wasn't fine, he thought, as he leaned a little closer, noticing how her usual elfin cheekiness had drained away. Now he saw the tension beneath the laughter, and realised that she no more let the world see inside her heart than he did himself.

Without warning she opened her eyes, looking straight at him. For a moment he was transfixed, more startled than she.

'I'm sorry,' he said at last, softly. 'I was worried about you.'

'Why?'

'You're not happy.'

'I'm all right.'

'*Are* you?'

She shook her head. Then she rubbed her eyes.

'What am I doing down here?' she asked, looking around.

'You don't remember?'

'Oh, yes, I stayed up late and fell asleep. I started looking around, and remembering everything about this place. It still looks almost exactly as it did when I first came here.'

She rose to her feet, but her limbs were cramped and

she moved awkwardly. He put out both hands to help her and she clung to him.

'What was it like then?' he asked.

'I thought it was magic—flagstones, open fireplace, little old-fashioned windows. When Mark walked into this room for the first time, it was like seeing myself again, full of a child's wonder.

'And it went on being wonderful when I grew up. I loved coming back here and being with Uncle Joe—all the happiest times of my life—and I wanted to keep it for ever, just as he kept it—'

Her voice had grown more and more husky until at last it ran out, and she passed a hand over her eyes.

'Look, we'll do something about it,' he said. 'Don't cry—'

'I'm not crying,' she flashed. 'I never cry.'

'So I see,' he murmured.

'It's just that—that dreadful woman will change everything. I don't want her to, but I can't stop her because it'll be hers and—it's all wrong.'

This time she buried her face in her hands, and her shoulders shook.

'I think perhaps you're crying,' he said kindly.

'No, I'm not—yes, I am—*oh, hell*!'

'Yes, that's usually the best thing to do,' he said, putting his arms about her so that her head fell naturally against his shoulder.

She left it there. She didn't want to argue any more. She just wanted to release all the tears she'd been holding back ever since she'd understood the extent of her loss.

He surprised her by being the perfect comforter, holding her patiently against the warm, strong column of his body while she wept. And she, a woman who prized her independence and detachment, clung to him as though he were her last hope.

But at last she began to feel self-conscious, and moved to disengage herself.

'I don't know what came over me,' she said awkwardly. 'I don't usually do that.'

'Perhaps you should do it more often.'

'Not me. I'm not the type,' she said firmly.

'Of course you're not. But you shouldn't try to do everything alone. Isn't there someone to help you?'

'I don't have any other family.'

'Then what about Andrew? Isn't he an accountant?'

'Yes, but—'

'Then why can't he think up some brilliant financial scheme—a tax dodge or something? What's the point of knowing an accountant if he can't fiddle the books for you?'

'I don't want him to fiddle anything.'

'But he should at least have offered.'

She remembered telling Andrew about the cottage. He'd advised her to hold out for the best price, but he hadn't thought of a way to help her keep it.

'Why not ask him?' Justin urged.

'I suppose I could. He'll be here any day.'

'Any day? How much time do you have?'

'None. You're right. I'll call him now. At this hour he'll be asleep.'

And it was the perfect excuse to call him and ask him when he was coming down. Seizing the phone, she dialled Andrew's London apartment. It rang for some time before he answered, sounding slightly muffled.

'Hallo, sleepyhead,' she teased.

She heard the moment of shocked silence but refused to understand it.

'Evie,' he said at last.

'Who did you think it was?' she asked, trying to laugh, although there was something inside her that wasn't laughing at all.

'I—well—I don't know.'

'I've been at the cottage a few days now. You're going to love it here, really.'

'Well—actually, I wanted to talk about that—I mean, the way things have been recently—'

He let his voice die away awkwardly, and in the silence Evie heard a sound that froze her blood.

A giggle.

It was definitely a giggle, not a laugh, or even a chuckle, but the giggle of a young woman who had been put in a very good mood by something or other.

'Come on, darling,' she cooed from close to Andrew. 'Don't stay on that phone for ever.'

Andrew spoke in a low, hurried voice.

'Evie, are you still there?'

'Oh, yes. I wouldn't miss this for anything.'

'I hope you're not going to be unreasonable. After all, it's usually you apologising to me—'

'Not for being caught out in bed with someone else.'

'Well—things haven't been going well for us, and I don't really think you mind about this—'

'Don't tell me what I mind and don't mind,' she said tensely.

'I'm sorry, but it's just a nice change to be with someone who puts me first. You never did that, and if you think over *why* you didn't, you'll realise that this isn't really such a big deal.'

She opened her mouth to put him right on this point, then closed it again. While she was choosing her words the line went dead. He'd hung up on her.

'Andrew? *Andrew!*'

She hung up, dazed by shock. Justin, coming out of the kitchen, where he'd retired to give her some privacy, saw her staring into space.

'No?' he asked gently.

'No.'

'He can't help you?'

'I didn't even ask him. It's over. He isn't coming here.' She gave a jerky laugh. 'I suppose he never really was, was he?'

'I don't think so,' Justin agreed gently.

'I'm a fool. I should have seen it all before. He was in bed with someone else.'

He came beside her. 'You really never suspected?'

'No,' she said with self-mockery. 'I've been so full of myself. I just saw it from my own point of view. We were going to have an idyllic time here, and I was going to tell him that I really did love him, and everything was going to be all right. But things don't work like that, do they?'

'No, I guess they don't.'

He touched her face, brushing her untidy hair back. 'Come on, Evie, you're not broken-hearted. You're not madly in love with him. You never were.'

'You're as bad as he is,' she said, incensed. 'Telling me how I feel.'

He made a wry face. 'When a woman's really in love it's pretty obvious. She never forgets the man for an instant. Can you honestly say that you never forgot Andrew? Be honest, Evie. You hardly remembered him.'

Now he'd gone too far. She made a move to free herself but his arms tightened. She gasped with outrage that he was daring to keep her prisoner.

'He didn't remember you either,' Justin continued remorselessly, 'because when a man loves a woman she's there with him, in his mind and his heart, every moment of the day.'

'Let me go—'

'Could you feel his body against you even when you were miles apart? Did the thought of him excite you? I don't think so.'

'How dare you—?'

She tried to struggle free again but it was useless. His face was close and she could feel his warm breath whispering past her cheeks, against her mouth. To her intense annoyance the sensation seemed to go right through her body, making her aware of him in a way that she would rather not have been at this moment.

'Did his kiss drive you wild, Evie, or don't you even remember that?'

She barely heard the last words, murmured as his mouth descended. She'd known what he meant to do but refused to believe it until his lips touched hers.

Even then she wouldn't face it. It wasn't possible that this awkward, arrogant, manipulative man should send shivers of excitement through her. It wasn't possible, *it wasn't possible!* She must hang on to that thought.

She tried to shut herself down and not be aware of her own feelings, but her body wouldn't let her off the hook. It insisted on responding to every sensation as his lips moved over hers again and again.

Her heart was a traitor too, pounding as it had never done before, almost as though it were in league with Justin. And while her mind seethed with indignation, her flesh ached for him to touch her more deeply, more intimately.

At last he loosened his grip enough for her to draw

back. She was breathing heavily with rage and something else.

'I'm warning you,' she gasped, 'if you don't let me go this minute, I'll do something that will make your ears ring for a week.'

Now he would lose his temper and she would have the satisfaction of a real knock down, drag 'em out fight. She was looking forward to it, every inch of her vibrating in anticipation, in a way that was new, violent and shocking.

But Justin disappointed her. There was no rage, no outburst. He just stood there looking dazed and confused.

'I'm sorry,' he said. 'I don't know what—I just wanted you to understand that this man—that you don't—'

'And I'm supposed to fall at your feet, am I?'

'No, that's—'

'You have the most unspeakable nerve. You think I have no feelings because that's what it suits you to believe. I've just lost the man I loved. I suppose the idea that I might be broken-hearted never occurred to you.'

'It might have done if you'd been a different woman,' he retorted.

'You have no idea what kind of woman I am.'

'I know you've got a lot of common sense—'

'Thanks a lot!' she snapped, insulted.

He threw up his hands. 'Now what have I said wrong?'

Since she couldn't have told him in a million years, she changed tack. But to be accused of common sense was a slur not to be forgiven.

'You seem to think you know everything about everybody, but this is my life. *I* decide how I feel—'

'You could if you were thinking straight,' he said. 'As it is, I'll spell it out for you. You're well rid of him. He was a waste of space.'

'You never even met him.'

'That's right, I haven't. And why? Because he isn't here when you need him. You were worried sick about losing your home, and what was he doing? Screwing around, that's what. He didn't do one single thing to help you.'

'It's not his problem—'

'Then it damned well ought to be.'

'Well, I confused him by sending out the wrong signals.'

'Give me patience!' Justin said in deep disgust. 'What happened to the independent woman I thought I knew?'

'She took the night off!'

'She's taken her whole life off if you're going to talk this way. Why must you blame yourself?'

'Have you never blamed yourself for anything?'

'Not if I could help it.'

'I can believe that.'

'Sometimes you have to admit you were wrong,' he admitted, 'but only a fool rushes into it.'

'Great! Now I'm a fool.'

'I won't answer that since everything I say seems to be wrong.'

'Hah! You noticed.'

She knew she was talking nonsense but her nerves were jangling.

'Look,' he said, with an air of exaggerated patience calculated to drive her to murder, 'I only kissed you. I was trying to make you feel better—'

'You conceited—'

'I mean by making you see things in a new light.

Maybe I did it clumsily—all right, yes, I was clumsy,
but I—oh hell!'

He turned away, tearing his hair, but almost immediately swung back to face her.

'Fine, I did it the wrong way. But if you could just
clear your head long enough to consider—'

'There you go again. Even your apologies are insults
in disguise—and not that deep a disguise—'

'If you don't shut up I'll kiss you again.'

'Now there's a threat that'll keep me silent for years.'

He drew a sharp breath. His face was full of fury and
for a moment she wondered if he would carry out his
threat.

But he didn't. Instead, he snatched up a towel where
he'd dropped it on a nearby chair and stormed out.

Evie ran upstairs. From her window she could watch
Justin run across the sand to the sea. He'd removed his
shirt, which was a pity because it brought back the sensation of being pressed against his bare chest.

She had never been so angry with him. Everything he
had done was inexcusable: trying to dictate to her, daring
to throw the light of common sense over her relationship
with Andrew, kissing her, not kissing her.

She threw herself on to her bed, trying to quell the
turbulence within. He was right. Of course he was right.
Hadn't she always known that her relationship with
Andrew was incomplete, because she'd always withheld
part of herself? Hadn't she driven Andrew into another
woman's arms, and secretly known what she was doing
all the time?

She heard Mark moving in the next room and forced
herself to be calm. By the time the boy came downstairs
she was there ahead of him, smiling and preparing
breakfast.

'Where's Dad?'

'He went for an early swim.'

'Can we go too?'

'Have some breakfast first.'

Justin came in a few minutes later, greeted them both, and said, 'I have to go away for a few hours today.'

Mark said nothing, but regarded his father with a face that was suddenly tense.

'Is that all right?' Justin asked, speaking to them both and neither in particular. If he was looking at anyone, it was Mark. But it was hard to be sure.

'That's fine,' Evie said. 'Mark and I will have a great day together, won't we, Mark?'

When he didn't answer she looked at him and found him staring fixedly at his father.

'Will you be away long, Dad?'

'Only until tomorrow.'

'Promise?'

'I promise,' he said, speaking gently. 'I'll be back tomorrow.'

'Where are you going?'

'That's a secret. But when I come back I'll have a surprise for you, and I think you'll like it.'

Mark nodded, seemingly satisfied. Justin ruffled his hair and went upstairs to change.

For a moment Evie was tempted to go after him, but she thought better of it. After a while he came downstairs, formally dressed, carrying a briefcase. This was a man intent on business, just as she had first known him.

Then she understood why Mark had asked if he were returning. He'd seen that, for his father, the holiday was over. In a few hours Justin would telephone, saying that he was staying in London and asking her to bring Mark home.

Fine! Evie thought with a touch of contempt. She wouldn't let his son down, even if he did.

They waved him off together and spent the day at the beach. Neither of them mentioned Justin. In the evening they played chess. Evie began by resolving to let Mark win a game or two, and ended up struggling to beat him even once. His twinkling eyes told her that he'd followed her thoughts.

She laughed with him, thinking how like Justin he looked. His mouth was different, gentler, with a touch of sweetness, but his nose was exactly the same, sharp and dominating his face, with a curiously flat bridge.

The phone rang. Mark ran to be the first to answer it.

'Hallo, Dad? When are you coming home? OK—I'll put you on to Evie—all right. I'll tell her.'

He replaced the receiver.

'Dad couldn't talk to you because he was in a hurry, but he says he'll be here first thing tomorrow.'

She answered vaguely. She was disturbed by a small knot of anxiety that was easing inside her, almost as though she were glad of his return. Even pleased, although pleased was perhaps going a bit far. She would admit to relief, but only for Mark's sake.

They tidied up and went to bed. Evie lay in the dark and tried to focus her attention on Andrew, wondering just how broken-hearted it was suitable for her to be. After a while she gave up. How could you grieve for a man whose face you couldn't remember?

In the early hours she awoke, hearing sounds from below. In a moment she was out of bed, pulling a light dressing gown on over her pyjamas and slipping quietly out on to the landing. The light was growing fast and she could see the man who had just arrived.

'Justin?' she called softly.

'Yes, come down. I have something to tell you.'

'Goodness, what's happened?' she asked, wondering at his businesslike tone.

She hurried down and saw him rummaging in his briefcase. He looked tired and unshaven.

'Have you been driving all night? You look done in.'

'Never mind that,' he said, sounding almost impatient. 'There's something I want you to see.'

'Is this the surprise you told Mark about? Shall I fetch him?'

'Later. I want you to see it first.'

'You're getting me worried.'

'No need. Here.' He'd found a large envelope in his briefcase and held it out to her. 'This is yours.'

'What is it?'

'Look at it,' he said curtly.

At first the words were a jumble, dancing before her eyes. Then she recognised the address of the cottage.

'It's sold,' she said at last. 'You mean the Nicholsons moved that fast?'

'Not them. Me. I bought this place yesterday.'

'You *what*?' Then her eyes fell on the price. *'How much?'*

The final price was fifty grand higher than the original asking price.

'You didn't really pay that?' she gasped.

'I had to. When the Nicholsons heard of my offer they raised theirs, which, I must admit I hadn't expected, considering that they tried to get it cheap. But, once they'd decided, they were determined not to let go. There was a bidding war, but I won because I kept going longer.'

'Yes, I can imagine that you did,' she said, dazed. 'But why—?'

'Look at the other paper. It'll tell you.'

The other paper was a deed of gift, making over the cottage to herself.

'I don't understand this,' she murmured.

'Surely it's clear enough? The cottage is yours. I bought it and now it's yours.'

She should have felt an uprush of gratitude, but there was only the old, uneasy feeling of a net closing about her. He hadn't done this for her sake, but for reasons of his own.

'But why are you giving it to me?' she asked.

His manner became even more impatient.

'What does it matter why? The point is, it's yours. You won't have to move out now. And since I paid over the odds you'll have plenty left when the debts are cleared. It's a very good deal for you.'

'Yes, it is, isn't it?' she said in a voice that was suddenly hard. 'And you really did pay over the odds, I can see.'

'Sometimes you have to, if it's the only way to get what you want.'

'I understand that,' she said slowly. 'It's really impressive, the way you never let anyone get the better of you. Not anybody. Ever.'

Something in her manner finally got through to him. He turned, regarding her with a puzzled frown.

'Evie, don't you understand? The cottage is yours. Yours to keep. For ever. It's what you wanted. Don't you have anything to say to me?'

She raised smouldering eyes to him.

'Yes,' she said fiercely, 'I do have something to say to you. *I shall never forgive you for this as long as I live.*'

CHAPTER SEVEN

JUSTIN stared at her. 'Did I hear that properly?'

'I think you did. What were you expecting? Gratitude? Well, maybe I'd be grateful if I didn't know the real reason behind this.'

His voice was hard. 'And you think the reason is what?'

'Control. Acquisition. I'm useful to you, because of Mark, and when something's useful you have to make sure it can't escape, right? So you buy it.'

He went pale. 'Is that what you think? That I'm trying to buy you?'

'What else? The perfect takeover bid, mounted under perfect conditions—the important one being secrecy so that the object of acquisition doesn't even know about it until it's too late.'

'Object of acquisition!' For pity's sake, listen to yourself! You're talking nonsense.'

'I don't think so. You've done a perfect job, behind my back, only I wasn't supposed to see the strings being pulled.'

'I tried to give you something,' he shouted. 'Something I thought you wanted. You've told me how much you love this place.'

'I was talking generally, not angling for a handout.'

'Yesterday you were crying about it.'

'Don't remind me about yesterday,' she said dangerously.

The way he'd kissed her as an assertion of power

102

rankled with her still, and drove her to lash him cruelly. She would think about it later. For now she only knew that the moment she had seen him her heart had felt a disturbance that was mysteriously linked to anger.

'The place is yours now,' he snapped. 'Do what you damned well like with it.'

'I can't. This isn't right. It mustn't happen.'

'You can't stop it. The sale's gone through.'

'I don't see how you can have done it in one day. All that money takes time.'

His shrug was a complete answer. What was a huge amount to her was a pittance to him. He'd probably handed over cash.

'I can't accept the cottage as a gift,' she said. 'Nor can I take the extra money. As soon as it's paid to the executor, and he's cleared the debts, I'll tell him to return you the balance.'

'That's ridiculous,' he shouted. 'Where's your common sense?'

'Obviously I don't have any. But I do have some self-respect, enough not to take charity from you.'

She heard his sharp intake of breath, and the look on his face was very ugly. She held out the papers and he snatched them.

'Go to hell,' he said with soft venom. 'Go there and stay there.'

Both tense with anger, neither noticed a figure looking down at them from the stairs, or heard the soft noise as he scuttled back to bed.

For a moment it seemed that Justin expected her to yield. When she didn't he simply walked out of the room, and a moment later she heard his car starting up. She sank down on the stairs, trembling violently.

She wondered what had come over her to have rejected his gift. To keep the cottage had been her heart's desire, and now it was hers, if she would only bend her pride a little.

But no power on earth could make her bend it for this man. His curt, businesslike tone as he'd outlined his methods, the way he'd crushed all opposition, the easy way he tossed money around, told her all she needed to know about his motives.

And it was all the worse because a corner of her heart had started to warm to him. If he'd done this in friendship she might have been tempted to accept. But Justin Dane didn't 'do' friendship.

She went back to her room and lay down, not expecting to sleep. But the fight had left her drained, and she dozed uneasily. When she awoke the sun was high, but Justin's car had not returned.

Looking out, she saw Mark sitting far out on the rocks. She dressed and hared out after him, ready with the words of reproach for slipping away alone. But they died on her lips when he raised his eyes and she saw the unhappiness in his face. Just like at the start, she remembered.

'Hallo,' she said, speaking cheerfully. 'You're out early. Anything interesting in the pool?'

'Some crabs. Nothing much. I just wanted to think a bit.'

'Well, it's a good place for it. Did you come up with anything?'

He shook his head. 'Thinking doesn't really help,' he said wistfully. 'It doesn't change anything.'

He was too young to believe that, she thought. Unable to find any words of wisdom she said, 'It's easier to think on a full stomach. Breakfast?'

He nodded. 'Then can we come back?'

'Yes, we'll spend the day here.'

She waited for him to ask if his father had returned, but he said nothing.

After breakfast they went back to the beach and explored the rock pools until Mark said, 'Here's Dad.'

Justin was coming across the sand towards them. He smiled at Mark, and then in Evie's general direction.

Mark greeted his father kindly but without eagerness. Nor did he ask about the surprise Justin had promised. She recalled his sadness of that morning and guessed that it was still there, suppressed beneath a polite smile.

It was like that for the rest of the day. On the surface all was calm. But beneath were tensions, only just held in check. In the evening Justin insisted on taking them out to a restaurant.

It was an expensive place and they all dressed up for it. She wondered why he'd done this until she realised that, in the fuss of waiters and choices to be made, the awkwardness between them was less noticeable.

He offered her wine, but refused it himself, explaining that he never touched alcohol.

Of course, she thought. Staying teetotal is a way of keeping control.

But then she castigated herself for dwelling so much on thoughts of him and his motives. There and then she made a resolution to put him out of her mind.

But that was hard when other people seemed so aware of him. At a nearby table sat two young women, both of whom seemed much taken with Justin. They regarded him with lustful appreciation, tried to catch his eye, smiled if his head turned briefly.

They were beauties that any man would be proud to have on his arm, and they were Justin's, if he wanted them, which he didn't seem to. She had to give him full marks for courtesy, for he gave her and Mark his whole attention.

She was forced to see him through their eyes as a vitally attractive man, with a presence and charisma that went beyond mere good looks, and she began to remember things she would rather forget: days on the beach with him stretched out beside her, half naked or fooling in the surf. From there it was a short step to being held against his bare chest as he kissed her fiercely, repeatedly.

It was useless to say that she hadn't wanted that kiss. Some part of her *had* wanted it, although she would go to the stake before letting him suspect.

Then came other thoughts—the way she'd awoken on the sofa to find him kneeling beside her, asking gently about her sadness. His unexpected kindness had touched her heart, making her vulnerable to him. But then he'd tried to turn it to his own advantage...

'Are you all right?' Mark asked her.

'I'm fine.'

'I thought you looked a little sad.'

'Not me,' she said untruthfully.

It was late when they reached home and Mark's eyelids were drooping. When Evie suggested that he go to bed he agreed without protest. Justin bade his son goodnight and immediately opened his computer.

'I think I'll go to bed, too,' she said.

'Fine,' he said. 'Goodnight.'

She regarded the back of his head with exasperation.

'Goodnight,' she said, and went upstairs.

She tucked Mark in and sat down on the bed. 'You didn't enjoy today, did you?' she asked.

He shook his head. 'It was like it used to be.'

'Used to be? When?'

'Just before Mum left. She and Dad—they were polite
but it was horrible.'

Evie groaned. Why hadn't she thought?

'I'm sorry, Mark. We were just both in a bad mood.
It didn't mean anything. Don't worry. Go to sleep, and
everything will be all right in the morning.'

But when she'd gone to bed and switched out her light
she wondered if she'd spoken truly. How could everything be all right after this?

She lay for a while, trying to get to sleep, but actually
listening for the sound of Justin climbing the stairs.
Instead she heard something from the next room that
made her sit up in bed. There it was again—a wail from
Mark's room.

She was out on the landing in a moment, pushing open
his door to find the child sitting up, his eyes closed, tears
pouring down his face.

'Mark,' she said urgently, taking him into her arms.
'What is it, darling?'

'Mum,' he wailed, 'Mum!'

She tightened her arms, feeling the frail body shaking
with misery against her. He'd given up on words now
and simply lay against her, crying uncontrollably. At last
she felt his hands grasping her arms tightly.

'I'm sorry,' he hiccuped.

'There's nothing to be sorry about. But please, tell me
what's the matter. Did you have a bad dream?'

'No, it was a lovely dream.'

'Was it about your mother?'

'Um!' He nodded against her shoulder.

'You miss her all the time, don't you?' she whispered.

'It's worse at night, because then I dream she's alive.
She comes home to me and says it was all a mistake
and she didn't mean to go without me. Then we run

away together. Or sometimes she stays home with me. It was a mistake, you see. She didn't really leave me because she wouldn't do that.'

His voice rose on the last few words and he buried his face against her, shaking with sobs.

'No, darling, she wouldn't,' Evie murmured, racked for him.

Gradually he grew quieter. She continued to sit there, holding and soothing him, but actually alert, because her sharp ears had detected a faint sound from just outside the door.

'She would have come for me,' Mark said, 'if she hadn't died.'

'Of course she would. And I know she never stopped thinking of you, all the time.'

'Really?'

'Yes, really.'

'Then why didn't she come home? Do you think Dad stopped her?'

'No,' she said swiftly. 'I know he wouldn't do that.'

'You don't really know.'

'Yes, I do. He'd never do anything to hurt you. Mark, you must believe me.'

'But he wouldn't bring her home when she died.'

'That's different. When she was alive—'

She paused. She had no right to repeat to Mark what Justin had told her. After a moment she realised that she had no need to say any more. The child had fallen asleep against her shoulder.

Gently she laid him down on the bed and drew the covers up. Then she kissed his cheek before slipping quietly out of the room and closing the door.

It was dark in the corridor, but the sliver of moonlight from the window was just enough to show her Justin standing there, leaning against the wall, his head back, motionless.

'Waiting at the window every week,' he whispered.

'Justin—'

'Standing there for hours because today would be different—today she'd really come.'

Of course he'd heard his son's words, and his heart had understood. If only he could talk directly to Mark like this. She could see the tears on his cheeks. He didn't try to brush them away. Perhaps he didn't know about them.

She reached out and held him, enfolding him in the same gesture she had used to comfort his son, and at once she felt his arms go around her, clinging on to her as if he were seeking refuge.

'But she never came—' he murmured.

'Justin!' She took hold of him, giving him a little shake.

He looked at her despairingly. 'I was sure she'd come, but she never did.'

'You?' she echoed, wondering if she'd heard him clearly.

'She promised,' he said huskily. 'I knew she wouldn't break her promise—but I never saw her again.'

Only then did she understand that Justin wasn't empathising with his son's loss. He was talking about a loss of his own.

It was as though a pit had opened beneath her, and from its depths came an aching misery that left her shattered. It clawed at her, howling of endless despair, grief too great to endure. The man in her arms was shuddering with that grief and she held him more tightly, helplessly trying to comfort something she did not understand.

They mustn't stay here, she thought. Mark might hear

them and come out. Gently she urged him across the
landing to her own room. He could barely walk.

Inside, she closed the door without switching on the
light. He almost fell on to the bed, taking her with him,
for his hands were holding on to her like grim death.

Once before he'd held her in an unbreakable grip, but
this was different. Instead of arrogance, she felt only his
need and desperation and everything in her went forward
to meet it, embrace and console it.

'It's all right,' she murmured, just as she had done
with the child. 'I'm here. Hold on to me.'

He kept his eyes fixed on her. He was still trembling
like a man caught in a nightmare from which there was
no escape.

'Justin, what's the matter? It's not just about Mark's
mother, is it?'

'No,' he said hoarsely.

'Tell me about it.'

'I can't—so many things—there's no help for it now.'

'There's help for everything, if you've got someone
who really wants to help you,' she said. 'But how can
I, if I don't understand?'

'How can you understand, when I don't understand it
myself?' he whispered. 'I want to ask why—I've always
wanted that—but there's nobody to ask.'

She couldn't bear his agony. Without thinking about
it, she leaned down and laid her lips tenderly over his.

'It's going to be all right,' she whispered. 'I'm going
to make it all right.'

She had no idea what she meant, or what she could
do to help him. But the details didn't matter. What mattered was easing his pain in any way she could. So she
kissed him again and again until she felt him begin to
relax in her arms.

It was unlike the other kiss in every way but one, and that was the slow burning inside her. But whereas that first excitement had been entwined with anger, this one was a part of pity and sorrow. She wanted him to find oblivion in her, lose himself in her completely, if that could give him a respite from suffering.

So she offered herself to him without reservation, waiting for the moment when his own desire rose and he reached out, taking over the kiss, turning her so that he was above her on the bed.

He checked himself for a moment, as though the earlier memory had come back to him. Seeing his doubt, she began to unbutton his shirt while her smile told him enough to ease the dread in his face. Then he was opening her pyjama top and laying his face against her warm skin.

He stayed like that for so long that she wondered if this was all he wanted, but then she felt his hands move on her with increasing urgency and she knew that they both wanted the same thing. And they wanted it now.

They made love quickly, as if trying to discover something they badly needed to know. And when they'd found the answer they made love again, but slowly this time, relishing the newly discovered treasure.

Afterwards there was peace, clinging to each other for safety in this new world, while the moonlight limned their nakedness.

She kissed him. 'Can you talk about it now?' she whispered.

'I'm not sure. I've never tried before.'

'Maybe that's the trouble. Talk to me, Justin, for both our sakes.'

'I don't know where to begin.'

'Start with your mother.'

'Which one?'

The answer startled her. She rose up on one elbow and looked down on him. After a moment he started to speak, hesitantly.

'For the first seven years of my life, I was like any other child. I had a home, two parents who loved me, or seemed to. Then the woman I thought of as my mother became pregnant.

'Almost overnight she lost interest in me. I found out why almost by chance. I overheard her talking to her sister, saying, 'It'll be wonderful to have a child of my own'. That was how I learned that she wasn't really my mother.'

'Dear God!' Evie said softly. 'Did you tell her what you'd heard?'

'No, I kept it to myself for months, pretending it wasn't true. But the pretence wore thin, especially when the baby was born, a boy.

'I was jealous. I started to have tantrums. So they called social services and said that I was "out of control" and I must go into care. After that I couldn't pretend any longer. I'd been adopted as second best, because they thought they couldn't have children. Now they didn't need me.'

She stared at him, too shocked to speak.

'I don't remember much about that day,' he said. 'I know I screamed at my parents not to send me away. I begged and pleaded but it was no use. They didn't want me.'

'Wait, stop,' she begged, covering her eyes as though, by this means, she could blot out the terrible story. 'I can't take this in. Surely they must have had some love for you?'

'You don't understand. I was a substitute. If they'd

never had one of their own I suppose they'd have made do with me, but now I was surplus to requirements. It took me years to see that, of course. All I knew at the time was that it was my own fault for being wicked.'

'How could anyone be so cruel as to put that burden on a child?' she burst out furiously. 'It's unspeakable. I suppose that's what *they* wanted to believe so that they didn't have to feel guilty about what they were really doing.'

'Yes, I worked that out in the end, too. But at the time I believed what I was told.'

'Where did they take you?'

'To what is laughingly known as a "home", which means an institution. At first I thought my mother would come and visit me. I used to stand at the window, watching the entrance. I *knew* she'd come. But weeks went by and there was no sign of them. Even then I didn't face it, not until one of the other boys jeered, "You're wasting yer time. Yer Mum dumped yer".

'Of course, then I knew, because in my heart I'd always known. The only way I could cope was to fight him. He was bigger than me, but I won because I hated him, not only because of what he'd said, but because his mother was taking him home the next day.

'The home wasn't a bad place. They meant well and they did their best. There was no affection because the staff turnover was so high, but I couldn't have dealt with that anyway. I'd learned enough not to want to get close to people, so I don't know what I'd have done if anyone had tried to get close to me. Something violent, probably.'

She shook her head in instinctive denial. At one time she might have mistaken him for a violent man, but now she sensed differently.

'I left when I was sixteen,' he resumed, 'and on the last day—'

He stopped, and a shudder went through him.

'What happened?' she asked softly.

He didn't answer at first. Then he said, 'Give me a minute.'

He rose and walked to the window. She stared at his broad back, wondering how she could ever have thought his size and strength alarming. All she could see now was that he was racked with misery. She went to stand beside him, turning him towards her, and had to fight back tears at what she saw.

He was actually shaking. Something was devastating him, and for a moment she thought he would be unable to speak of it.

At last he said, 'When I left they had to tell me the whole truth about myself. That was when I learned that my birth mother had given me away almost as soon as I was born.'

Evie stared at him, slowly shaking her head in speechless horror.

His laugh was harsh and bitter.

'You'll hardly believe this, but I was left on the orphanage doorstep like some Victorian foundling. If your mother does that, she can't be traced, you see. She's got rid of you completely.

'That was all they knew. I turned up one evening out of the blue. Apparently a doctor said I was about a week old. They did some research into the babies that had been born recently in that area, but none of them was me.'

'You mean your birth wasn't even registered?'

'Not by my mother. The orphanage registered me, of course.'

'It's awful,' she whispered. 'All this time, not know-ing who you really are.'

'But I do know who I am,' he said with bitter irony. 'I'm the son two mothers didn't want. What could be clearer than that?'

'I used to wonder why you were so angry and sus-picious all the time,' she said. 'Now I wonder how you've managed to keep your head together.'

'I'm not sure I have. For a long time I was crazy. I didn't behave well, either in the home or after I'd left it. I drank too much, brawled, got into trouble with the police, served some time in jail. That brought me back into contact with my adoptive parents.'

'They came to help you?' she asked, longing for some redeeming moment in this dreadful story.

'No, they sent a lawyer to say they'd get me a good defence on condition that I stopped using their name. They had an unusual name, Strassne, and since I still bore it people were beginning to associate this young low-life with them.'

'So that was when you became Justin Dane?' she asked. She would have liked to say something more vi-olent, but was controlling herself with a huge effort.

'No, I became John Davis. My one-time ''parents'' insisted on doing it by deed poll, so that it was official and they'd never have to acknowledge me again. Then they paid for a very expensive defence, and John Davis was acquitted. They didn't even attend the trial.'

'So what happened to John Davis?'

'He didn't survive the day. I changed my name to Leo Holman. Not by deed poll. I just took off and gave my name as Leo wherever I went.'

'Don't you need some paperwork to get things like passports and bank accounts?'

'Yes, and if I'd needed those things it would have been a problem, but I wasn't living in a world of passports and bank accounts. I worked as a handyman, strictly for cash, got into trouble again, went inside— never long sentences, just a couple of months, but every time I came out I changed my name again. I lost track of how often. What did it matter to me? I no longer had a real identity, so it didn't matter how often I changed it.

'The last time I was in prison I met a man who put me straight. His name was Bill. He was a prison visitor, but he'd done time himself so he knew what he was talking about. He saw something in me that could be put back on track, and he set himself to do it.

'When I came out he was there waiting for me. He gave me a room in his own house, so that he could watch me like a hawk to see that I stayed on the straight and narrow. And he made me go to evening classes. I learned things and I found that I enjoyed having ambitions. Bit by bit I turned into a respectable citizen, the kind of man who needs paperwork.

'So I changed my name one last time. I was Andrew Lester at that time and I turned into Justin Dane. I did it officially, by deed poll, and I went to work in Bill's firm.'

'How did you choose the name?'

'Bill had a Great Dane I enjoyed fooling with. I forget where Justin came from. In the end he loaned me the money to start my own business. In three years I repaid him. In eight years I bought him out. Don't misunderstand that. He was delighted. I gave him a good price, enough to retire on. I wouldn't have done him down. I owed him, and I repaid him.

'After that I just made money. It was all I knew how to do. I didn't seem able to make relationships work.'

'What about your wife? You must have loved her?'

'I loved her a lot. I even told myself that she loved me, but we married because she was pregnant and I wanted a child badly. But it didn't work out. In the end she couldn't stand me. She said so. The only good thing to come out of it was Mark.

'I thought with him, at least, I could make a success, but I haven't. I don't know how. I'm driving him away as I seem to drive everyone away.'

'But what happened with your mothers—either of them—wasn't your fault,' she urged. 'It couldn't be.'

'Maybe not, but it started me on a track I don't know how to escape.' He gave a soft mirthless laugh. 'You'll hardly believe this, but when people tell me to get lost I feel almost relieved. At least it's familiar territory.'

He fell silent. Evie slipped her arms about him and leaned against his body as they stood there in the window. But she too said nothing, because in the face of such a terrible story there was nothing to say.

CHAPTER EIGHT

AFTER that they didn't speak of it again. He had said as much as he could bear to, and Evie's instincts told her to leave it. She must start getting to know this man again from the beginning.

Everything she had thought true about him was now reversed. Instead of the harsh bully, manipulating her for ulterior motives, there was a forlorn child desperately wondering what he'd done wrong to be so unloved. That child would remain a part of him all his life, making him so vulnerable to slights and rejections that he could only cope by being the first to attack.

She smiled to think how annoyed it would make him to be seen in this light. It was something she would have to keep to herself.

They didn't tell Mark why the atmosphere had suddenly become happier, and he never mentioned the nights he awoke to find Justin's bed empty, and went contentedly back to sleep. His air of strain fell away and he smiled more, but, like his father, he knew how to keep his own counsel.

One night, as they lay peacefully in bed, Justin said, 'So what was all that about Andrew?'

She gave a gasp of laughter.

'Don't remind me what a fool I was. I guess I wanted to believe I was in love with him, and the effort to convince myself was tying me in knots.'

'But why?'

'You once said that no man had ever offered me life-time commitment—'

'I once said a lot of tomfool things. You shouldn't listen to me.'

'I try not to, but you're hard to shut out when you get going,' she said indignantly. 'And you really annoyed me that time, talking as though I'm some Victorian wall-flower grasping at her last chance. I'd kick you if I had the energy.'

He grinned and kissed her. 'So what's the real story?'

'I've always been the one fleeing commitment. It sounded so boring. I love my life, the freedom, the variety—'

'The motorbike.'

'Yup. There was never a man who made me want to change it, but I thought, if I waited long enough, I'd meet one. And suddenly I was nearly thirty and Andrew was such a sweet guy that I—well—'

'You decided he'd "do".'

'You make it sound terrible, but yes, I suppose that's true. I was starting to feel lonely, so I decided on Andrew. But I was always forcing it, and of course he knew something was wrong.'

'When you'd stood him up often enough he got the message?' Justin said with the amiable derision of the conqueror for his defeated rival.

'Well, I'm glad he did, and found someone who suits him better.'

'You can't be sure he has.'

She gave a soft chuckle. 'Yes, I can. Anyone would suit him better than me, and that girl sounded as though he'd made her *very* happy.'

They lay in sleepy contentment for a while. She was wondering how to broach the subject on her mind. At last she murmured, 'Have you told Mark that you bought the cottage?'

'No. I wasn't sure what to say, when you were so mad at me.'

'Only because I misunderstood. I thought you were— never mind. I was wrong. I heard from the lawyer this morning. He's paid all Uncle Joe's debts and sent me a cheque for the balance.'

'So I suppose you're going to throw that back at me?' His tone was deceptively light, but now she could hear the dread beneath.

'Nope,' she said cheerfully, snuggling up to him. 'I'm going to put it in the bank and make whoopee!'

'I'm glad.'

'Seriously, I'll use it to do some repairs to the cottage—that is—if it's still mine.'

He'd seized her into his arms before she'd finished speaking, using his mouth to incite and tease her towards what they both now wanted. But through his desire she also sensed passionate relief that she had finally accepted his offering, taking the sting out of her earlier rejection.

It would be good to believe that the revelations had made everything right, or at least given her the key to helping him. With her he'd found a kind of happiness, but that alone could not slay the demons of dread and insecurity that were devouring him inside. The darkness was not so easily defeated.

He still flared up about small things. His temper always died quickly, and he would apologise in a way that revealed his fear that he'd drive her away. She forgave him readily, but she worried about him.

Even more troubling were the times that he controlled his inner turbulence and went away to suffer alone, returning with a bright smile and an air of strain.

Once, when Mark had gone to bed and a chilly spell had made them light the log fire and stretch out on the old sofa before it, she asked him, 'Justin, how long can you go on like this?'

He shrugged. At one time it would have seemed dismissive, but now she understood his confusion.

'As long as there is,' he said. 'What else can I do?'

'The first time I saw you I thought how angry you were. As I came to know you better I realised that you were angry all the time. No matter what happens it's always there below the surface, waiting for something to trigger it, never giving you any peace.'

'I'm sorry I lost it today—'

'That's all right. You said sorry at the time, and you bought Mark that computer game to make up for it.'

'Yes, and he put it on my computer and I couldn't get to it for hours,' he said with resignation. 'Be fair, I didn't lose my temper about that.'

'No, you showed the patience of a saint. You even let him teach you the game and beat you.'

He managed a faint grin. 'I didn't *let* him beat me. He beat me. And he enjoyed crowing at my expense. He's a great kid, Evie. I even think—'

'No,' she said urgently. 'You're not going to change the subject. It's you we're talking about. You're not happy—'

'Yes, I am,' he said, tightening his arms about her. 'A little more of Dr Evie's Magic Balm and I'll be sweetness and light all the time.'

'Not in a million years! Besides, I don't think I'd like you as sweetness and light. I wouldn't recognise you, for one thing.' He gave a muffled laugh against her hair. 'Besides, a magic balm only works on the outside. You need something to work on the inside.'

'Evie, I'm not ill.'

'You're being devoured alive, and that's a kind of sickness.'

'You do the psycho-babble very well,' he said lightly.

But she would not let him put her off. 'Stop that,' she said urgently. 'I know what you're trying to do.'

'You know everything, don't you?'

'I said stop it. You're trying to distract me because you don't want to confront it.'

'All right, I don't,' he growled. 'Why the hell should I want to?'

'Because you'll never resolve it otherwise.'

'What is there to resolve? It's the situation. It's my life. It can't *be* resolved.'

'Maybe it can.'

'Evie, listen. I know you mean well, but you have to play the hand you're dealt. You can play it well or badly, but you can't change the hand you start with.'

'But you can investigate it. And then, maybe, you'll discover you weren't dealt the hand you thought.'

'What do you mean by that?'

'I mean you should find out about your real mother, who she was, and why she couldn't keep you.'

He stared at her. 'Are you crazy?'

'No, but you might be if you try to carry this burden any longer. I think you're already starting to break under it.'

It was a risky thing to say. She waited. He gave her a black look, but he didn't deny it.

'Haven't you ever tried to find her?'

'Why would I want to find her?' he growled. 'So that I can say, ''Hey, why did you toss me out with the junk? C'mon tell me, and that'll make it all right''?'

'But there might be things she could tell you that

would make you understand her better. Perhaps she had no choice. She was probably a young unmarried mother and it was very much harder for them in those days. At least try. It might make more difference than you think.'

'How could it? She gave me up. There's no way past that.'

'There is if she didn't *want* to give you up. She might have been pressured beyond endurance.'

'I'd like to see anyone try to pressure me to give up my son.'

'*Don't be ridiculous!*' she blazed. 'That is absolutely the stupidest thing I have ever heard anyone say. We're talking about a vulnerable girl. You're a grown man at the height of his powers. Nobody can bully you.'

'You're not doing badly.'

'I'm not bullying you, I'm just pointing out facts.'

'Right now I'm not sure there's a difference,' he said, eyeing her cautiously.

'Just because you can stand up to people it doesn't mean everyone else can. Honestly, Justin, that remark was plain idiotic.'

'All right,' he said harshly. 'I admit it. I was trying to get you off the subject. Do you think I want to let strangers poke and pry into my private life? Can you imagine how hard it was even to tell you? Suppose she wasn't a vulnerable girl. Suppose she was someone who just didn't want to bother.'

'All right, it's possible, but then I don't think she'd have given her baby away in secret. She'd simply have called social services. But neither of us really knows. That's why it's vital to find out.'

'You're forgetting that she never registered my birth. In a sense I never existed. All those agencies for re-

uniting people with their mothers can't help a man
whose mother's name isn't on his birth certificate.'

'That's going to make it more difficult,' she conceded.
'But not impossible. I've got a friend that I'd like to
give this to. He's a private detective, and he's brilliant.'

He was silent, racked by doubt. Evie could almost feel
the violence of his feelings tearing him in opposite directions.

'I can see to everything,' she urged. 'You give me all
the details and I'll talk to him. You won't even have to
meet him if you don't want to.'

'All right,' he said softly. 'If I can leave everything
in your hands, I'll do it.'

She held him close, praying that she'd done the right
thing for him. If it turned out badly, she might have
made his troubles a thousand times worse. But she knew
that he couldn't go much longer.

It was time to leave the cottage and return to London.
Evie took a last look around, thinking of how she'd arrived here meaning to pack up and say goodbye. And
now there were to be no sad goodbyes. At least, not to
the cottage. What the road ahead held for her and Justin
she could not tell.

So that they could travel together he arranged for a
driver to collect her van. As they drove home he said,
'It'll be very late when we reach London. Why don't
you stay with us tonight, or maybe a few days?'

And she said that would be lovely, almost as though
they hadn't planned it between them earlier. Mark
grinned. He was a child who saw and understood a lot
more than he was told.

Justin left for New York a couple of days later. Before
going he showed Evie his office and all the files that

concerned his birth. They were pitifully few, but they were a start.

When Justin had gone she contacted David Hallam, the private investigator who was a good friend.

'You're not giving me much,' he complained when he saw the material. 'Never mind. It'll be a challenge.'

On the night before Justin was due home David called her and said, 'You've really stirred things up.'

'You don't mean you've found something?'

He told her what he'd discovered, and she could barely contain her excitement. But she must be patient. She and Mark went to meet Justin at the airport, and she held back, letting the moment belong to father and son. Her time would come.

It came later that night when they were finally alone.

'I don't know how much it amounts to,' she said, 'but David has someone he wants you to meet.'

He tensed. 'Not—?'

'No, not her. A man. His name is Primo Rinucci, and his English stepmother had a son who was taken away from her at birth. For years he's been trying to find him for her. He's had feelers out with dozens of organisations and detective agencies, asking them to tell him if anyone with the right details contacted them. There's a chance that you're the man he's seeking.'

He turned pale. 'Dear God!'

'Justin, just think. If this works out, it means that *she's* been looking for *you*.'

'Don't!' he said in a harsh whisper. 'Don't encourage me to hope. *Evie!*'

'Yes, darling. Yes, *yes!*'

This might be the answer that would make him complete at last, and if they did not pursue it the doubt would torment them both. But she knew also that Justin was standing on a dangerous edge, and disappointed hope could destroy him. If that happened she would blame herself for ever.

'What else do you know about this man?' he asked.

'He comes from Naples and he's flying over here to meet you. I've provisionally set it up for the day after tomorrow.'

'I've got a meeting—'

'*Change it.*'

'Where do we go?'

'You want me to come with you?'

'I can't do it without you. Sometimes I don't think I can do anything without you. It's as though you're what links me to life. If that link were broken I'd just—' he fought for the words '—sink into a black hole and never come out again.'

It dawned on her that he was making what, in any other man, she would have called a declaration of love. But this man did nothing like the others.

He saw the understanding in her face and spoke in self-mockery.

'I'm making a pig's ear of it, aren't I?'

'Not really,' she said, smiling. 'I'm getting the message.'

'I'm glad, because there are some things—I can't do the "three little words" stuff.' He sounded desperate.

He might never say that he loved her, she realised. But her life had been full of men who could do the 'three little words stuff' easily, and she had wanted none of them. What she wanted was this clumsy bear of a man with his tortured, painfully expressed need.

'Do you remember the evening we collected Mark from the cemetery and you came home for supper?' he asked. 'The dogs were there, and their carry-on made you laugh.'

'Yes, I remember.'

'I'd never heard anyone laugh like that—such a sound—rich and warm—as though you'd found the secret of life. It seemed to—I had to follow—' he grimaced '—whether you wanted me or not.'

'A takeover bid,' she said, smiling fondly.

'Are you making fun of me?' He said it, not aggressively, but almost meekly, like someone who was trying to learn.

'Maybe just a bit,' she said, touching his face.

'You're being unfair. I do know that women are different from stocks and shares—'

'If only you could work out exactly how,' she teased.

He weaved his fingers through hers, drawing her hand to his lips, then resting it against his cheek.

'Laugh at me if you like,' he said, 'as long as you don't leave me.'

The meeting was set up in neutral territory. David hired a room in a London hotel and the four of them met for lunch, Evie carrying the file with all the paperwork.

Primo Rinucci turned out to be a tall man with slightly shaggy mid-brown hair, in his early thirties. Despite his name he spoke perfect English, with no trace of an accent.

Evie was prepared for anything, but in fact the truth was clear almost at once. When Primo first set eyes on Justin a stillness came over him and he drew a long breath. After that she knew.

She couldn't tell whether Justin had seen and understood. His manner was stiff and awkward and he scowled more than he smiled. David, with blessed tact, departed almost as soon as the introductions were made.

'Give me a call later,' he whispered to Evie.

When he'd gone the two men regarded each other warily.

'You are wondering what I can have to do with you,' Primo said. 'Let me tell you a little about myself. I was born in England and lived here for the first few years of my life. My father's name was Jack Cayman. He was English. My mother was Italian, and her maiden name was Rinucci.

'She died while I was a baby and my father married again, a young English girl called Hope Martin. She was a wonderful person, more a mother to me than a step-mother. Sadly, the marriage didn't last. When they divorced, my father insisted that I remain with him. Later he died. I went to Italy to live with my mother's parents, and took their name.

'But then Hope, my stepmother, learned where I was and came to see me. My family welcomed her, and my Uncle Toni fell in love with her. I was very happy when they married, especially as I was able to live with them. I felt I had regained my mother.

'It was years later, when I had grown up, that I learned that she'd had a child before her marriage to my father. She was only fifteen and her parents wanted her to give up her baby for adoption. They were furious when she refused.

'In the event she never even saw her child. They told her it had been born dead, which was a lie. It was a home birth and the midwife was her aunt. She took the boy away to another town, many miles away. Hope knew nothing about it.'

Justin said nothing, only stared hard at Primo. It was Evie who exclaimed in horror at what she'd just heard.

'Yes, it was wicked,' Primo said, looking at her warmly. 'Hope grieved for her "dead" child, but she grieved a thousand times more to think that he was alive and living apart from her, perhaps thinking she had abandoned him.'

Justin gave a small, convulsive jerk, but he didn't speak.

'How did she find out?' Evie asked.

'The aunt died. At the end she sent for Hope and tried to tell her what had happened, but she was too near the end to make much sense. Hope understood that her child had lived, had been stolen, and nothing else. She didn't even have the name of the town, because the aunt had gone to a place where she wasn't known. Apart from that, all she had was the date of his birth. This.'

He pushed a scrap of paper across the table. The date written on it was exactly two weeks before the date on Justin's official birth certificate.

'I began looking for him fifteen years ago,' Primo resumed. 'It took years to find the place where a baby boy had been abandoned soon after this date. At last my investigators narrowed it down to one possibility. Then I thought the search was over because this boy had been adopted by a couple called Strassne.'

There was silence in the room for a moment. Justin did not speak, but his grip on Evie's hand became painful.

'For several years he lived with them as Peter Strassne,' Primo said. 'But he assumed a new identity twenty years ago, and that was when the trail went cold. The deed poll said that Peter Strassne had become Frank Davis, but nobody ever heard of Frank Davis after that.'

Because he'd changed his name again, Evie thought
sadly. *And then again and again. And every time the
trail grew a little colder. By the time he became Justin
Dane there was nothing left to link him with his earlier
identities.*

'Once he'd seemingly vanished into thin air,' Primo
resumed, 'my only hope was if he too was searching,
and I might pick up his search. That is why I am here.
I think I already know the answer, but will you tell me
if your name was ever Peter Strassne?'

Slowly Justin nodded his head. Then he pushed the
file of papers across the table. Primo examined it briefly,
and nodded.

'I am satisfied,' he said.

'As easy as that?' Justin asked hoarsely. 'What can a
few papers prove?'

'I told you I already knew the answer. I knew as soon
as I saw you. Your resemblance to your mother is remarkable. There are tests that can establish your blood
tie once and for all, but there is no doubt in my mind
that you are Hope Rinucci's firstborn son.'

CHAPTER NINE

THE London to Naples flight left early, so the three of them spent the previous night in the airport hotel.

'Uncle Toni knows why I'm here,' Primo said as they sat over dinner the night before. 'But I didn't say anything to Mamma before I left, for fear of raising her hopes. But now I've called him and told him everything, and he's going to prepare her gently. She's dreamed of this for so long that the reality is going to come as a shock to her.'

'Will the whole family be there?' Evie wanted to know.

'Everyone, but for a while the others will stay out of sight.' He addressed Justin. 'The two of you will need to have your first meeting in private. Then we'll all gather.'

'Hope really has five other sons?' Evie asked.

'That's right, although not all of us were born to her. She and my father adopted Luke. Then there's Francesco. She fell in love with his father, Franco, while still married to Jack Cayman, which is really why my father divorced her. Carlo and Ruggiero are her sons by Toni.' He gave Justin an encouraging smile. 'So you have five brothers, one way or another.'

He didn't seem to notice that Justin's smile was faint and he'd spoken very little. He went on, 'Then Mamma will want to meet your son, Mark, her grandson. She'll be disappointed that he's not with you, but you were probably wise to leave him behind this time.'

'I'd like to get things sorted out first,' Justin said quietly.

'Of course. Signorina—' He turned to Evie and said in Italian, 'I'm delighted that you speak my language.'

'Only Italian,' she said in the same language. 'Not Neapolitan, except for a few words. But I want to learn more of your dialect.'

'I shall delight in teaching you.' He saw Justin frowning and said quickly in English, 'Forgive me. I'm being rude in using a language that you don't understand, but it's such a pleasure to discover a lady who speaks Italian so well. She will be a great help to you.'

He drained his glass.

'I think I'll have an early night.' Rising, he kissed Evie's hand, saying in Italian, *'Buona notte, moglie del mio fratello.'*

He departed.

Justin regarded her. After a moment he said edgily, 'Aren't you going to tell me what he said?'

'He just wished me goodnight,' she said hastily.

'No, he said more than that. Why should you conceal it?'

'Because it's a bit embarrassing. He called me his sister-in-law—wife of my brother. Forget it. I'm going to bed.'

He went up with her and they said goodnight at her door. But his knock came soon after.

'Are you all right?' she asked, letting him in. 'You've been very quiet all evening.'

He didn't reply at first, but walked about the room before saying abruptly, 'Evie, let's forget all this and go home.'

'You can't mean that, not after we've come this far.

You couldn't go away now, just when you're on the verge of discovering everything.'

'Am I? What is "everything"? Can you tell me that? At one time I might have agreed with you, but now I've met you I have another "everything". What connection can there be between her and me after all these years?'

'But you can't do that to her. She's expecting you now; it'll break her heart if you don't arrive. And in the years to come you'll regret not meeting her and finding out what you need to know. Justin, you're just making excuses—finding reasons. Why?'

He gave her a faint smile.

'You always see through me. Of course I'm making excuses. Because I'm afraid. I always thought of myself as strong. You have to make people see you like that because if they sense weakness they go in for the kill. But the truth is that I'm a coward and I've only just discovered it.'

'Don't be so hard on yourself. You're not a coward.'

'You know my weaknesses better than anyone, and you're the only person I could say that to, the only person I could trust that much. You're all I need. I want to spend my life with you. Nothing else matters.'

She smiled and touched his face tenderly.

'Darling, I love you, and it's wonderful that you say that, but—don't you see, we can't think about it now? What's going to happen tomorrow is so overwhelming that it's going to blot out everything else for a while. I'm here if you want me, but we can only go forward, not back.'

He nodded. 'Nothing could blot you out. I'll go forward if I have your hand in mine. Help me, Evie. With you I think I can manage anything. Without you—' His face clouded.

'But you don't have to be without me,' she said, taking him into her arms.

They made love tenderly, with her taking the initiative. She had never felt so strongly protective of him as at this moment.

Yet she could not ignore a small shadow at the back of her mind. He'd said he wanted to spend the rest of his life with her. It wasn't exactly a proposal, but she knew she could have turned it into one, had she wished.

Why hadn't she done so? Was it the old caution, that had held her back from marriage so often before? Or was it something more, something dangerous about this man, that warned her to beware, even while she felt the bands that linked her to him tighten around her heart?

The flight to Naples next morning went smoothly, and by early afternoon they were in the car sent to convey them to the Villa Rinucci.

Evie was so entranced to be back in Italy, and in a region that she'd always longed to explore, that she almost forgot everything else. It was the height of summer and the sun poured down over them as they took the coast road, then climbed up to the villa, with the Bay of Naples falling away below them.

Her first sight of the Villa Rinucci was pure magic. Seen from below, it was like a mini-palace made of honey-coloured stone. There were several wings and around the whole building was a covered terrace, the roof supported by high arches.

Looking out of the window, Evie thought she saw the figure of a tall, slender woman standing on the terrace, looking down at the car climbing the road. But the dazzling sun made her blink, and when she looked again the terrace was empty.

At last the car came to a halt in the courtyard on the other side of the house. A man was standing there.

'That is my Uncle Toni, and Mamma's husband,' Primo explained.

He was out of the car first, going forward to take his uncle's hand, then looking back to where Justin was getting out of the car, indicating him.

And there it was again, the slight start of astonishment as Toni Rinucci saw his wife's features in her son.

Primo introduced them quietly to each other, the men murmured something and Toni ushered them all towards the villa. As they approached, Evie could see faces at the windows and guessed these were some of the other sons, hovering nearby, but keeping a discreet distance.

When they were inside the villa, Toni Rinucci studied Justin more closely for a moment.

'Yes,' he said at last. 'Primo has assured us that you are the one, and now I see that he is right. If I did not believe that I would not let you near my wife. Since I told her she has been much disturbed, but she longs to see you. She is waiting for you in that room.'

Justin glanced at Evie, but she stepped back.

'This is just you and her,' she said. And he nodded.

Toni opened a door. Inside, a woman was sitting by a large window. The light was behind her, making her a silhouette. She rose as Justin entered, and Evie had a glimpse of the two of them moving slowly towards each other. A pause. Then Hope Rinucci's hands flew to her mouth in a gesture of joyful astonishment. And then they were in each other's arms.

Gently Toni closed the door.

'Signorina Evie,' he said, smiling, 'forgive me for not welcoming you properly before. Please believe that you are welcome in our home.'

He opened his arms in a huge Italian hug and she felt herself engulfed.

'My wife's maid will show you to your room,' he said when she finally came up, gasping for air. 'When you are ready, you will come down and meet some of the louts who hang around this house.'

There was muffled laughter from the gaggle of young men who had come downstairs but were still keeping a respectful distance, doubtless obeying orders.

Maria, the maid, showed her upstairs. Evie had an impression of a spacious building with warm red and brown flagstones, furnished in traditional style, with a great deal of polished wood. The effect was rustic, she noted, but the kind of elegant rustic that would take a great deal of money.

When she had freshened up Primo came to escort her downstairs, where Toni hugged her again.

'Primo has told us everything,' he said. 'How you helped and encouraged Justin in the search. My wife shall know of it. For now, you must have food and wine, and soon you will meet her.'

He led her out on to the terrace overlooking the bay and she stood gazing in wonder at the beauty until Toni offered her a glass of *prosecco*, the lightest possible sparkling white wine.

Now the other sons came forward to be introduced— Luke, the adopted one; Francesco, the love child; Carlo and Ruggiero, the twins, in their late twenties, full of zest and young, masculine attraction. Although not identical, they were sufficiently alike to show that they were brothers.

They plied her with questions about Justin, while contriving to make it clear that they admired her for their own sake. Ruggiero winked and gave her a soft wolf whistle, which prompted Carlo to say sharply, 'Mind your manners.'

He spoke in Italian and Evie immediately said in the same language, 'It's all right.'

That delighted them, and after that everyone spoke Italian. They were impressed by her and said so openly. Now the questions were about her, although only Ruggiero had the effrontery to look at her left hand and say, 'Then you aren't married to Justin? There's hope for the rest of us?'

'Behave yourself!' his father growled.

Ruggiero fell silent, but there was nothing meek in his demeanour and he gave Evie a conspiratorial wink.

A charmer and a ladies' man, she thought. He'll flirt with every girl in sight and it'll mean nothing. But he's harmless and likeable.

'Primo spoke as though you were already our sister-in-law,' Francesco explained.

'I've only known Justin a few weeks,' Evie said.

'But it was you who helped to set his feet on the road that led here,' Toni said. 'And it is you he chose to bring here with him. That means that in his heart you are his wife.' He raised his voice to add, 'And you will be treated as such by every man here.'

There were murmurs of, '*Si, Pappa.*' Toni turned back to her.

'If any of my sons offends you, please inform me at once, Signorina, and I will personally beat him black and blue.'

'I'm sure that won't be necessary,' she assured him, chuckling.

An hour passed, during which Evie made friends with them all. She was at ease and comfortable among these people. If only Justin could feel the same.

She thought of him, with Hope, the mother who had influenced his whole life by not being part of it. How was he coping?

At last there was a noise from outside. Someone hissed, 'They're coming,' and the next moment Hope Rinucci appeared, her hand tucked in Justin's arm. Together they came out on to the terrace.

Hope reached out to her husband, smiling through tears.

'He came back to me, Toni,' she said. 'He came back, as I always knew he would.'

'Of course he did, *carissima*,' he soothed her.

Justin kept his eyes fixed on his mother, as though what was happening had left him dazed. Evie tried to imagine what this moment meant to him, but it was beyond imagining.

She studied his face, seeking some sign of emotion, but she saw nothing. His expression was set and slightly fierce, much as it had been when he'd first told her his story.

She'd been partly expecting this. Justin would die before letting the world know how he felt. Even with her he found it hard. But surely she knew him well enough to read the signs?

Then, with a start of dismay, she realised that there were no signs. His face was the blank of a man who didn't even know what his feelings were.

At last he met her eyes and she saw his confusion. Years of dreading rejection had left him unable to react. She smiled back, trying to reassure him that it would happen later, when he wasn't under a spotlight.

But at this supreme moment, when there should be

joy and triumph, he was once more shut out and her heart ached for him.

Now that she saw Hope more clearly Evie understood why Justin had found instant acceptance. As Primo had said, the family resemblance was remarkable.

Carlo and Ruggiero studied their new brother with interest before shaking his hand. Then the others all offered their hands, signifying acceptance.

'Now,' Hope said, looking around at them, 'now I have all my sons beside me.'

Toni drew Evie forward to be introduced. Hope received her charmingly, but Evie didn't miss the shrewdness in the clear blue eyes, and knew she was being carefully inspected. She wondered what Justin had told his mother about her, and longed for a moment to talk to him.

It was a long time before such a moment came. Hope herself showed him to his room, clinging to his arm in a manner that Evie was glad to see. Nothing would do Justin more good than to have his mother claim him possessively like this. She dared to hope that soon his demons might be stilled.

She spent the rest of the afternoon with the twins, learning Neapolitan words. Then Toni showed her his library and she delighted him by studying his antique Italian books with real interest, and being able to translate them.

'You are an expert in my language,' he said, beaming.

'I hope so. It's how I earn my living, plus French, of course.'

'Pooh! French!' he said, dismissing a thousand years of French culture with a wave of an Italian hand. 'But

Italian—ah, wait until you see the people I can take you to meet. How I look forward to you being part of this family.'

'Please—' she said hastily.

'Of course,' he said, throwing up a hand. 'I understand that it's a delicate matter. I will say no more.'

The whole family joined up again for dinner that night. Justin sat beside Hope, who engaged him deep in conversation. Evie was glad to see that there was now less constraint in his manner. He could smile at his mother and speak naturally to her.

'When will I meet your son?' Hope asked him. 'My first grandchild. Indeed my only grandchild until another of my sons does his duty, which, I have to say, shows no sign of happening.'

There were grins and disclaimers around the table. Evidently this was an old bone of contention.

'Send for him,' Hope said. 'Bring him here tomorrow.'

It was charmingly said, with a radiant smile at Justin, but Evie noticed the hint of command. This was a woman used to announcing what she wanted and having her wishes fulfilled.

'Tomorrow's a little soon,' Justin said. 'I shall have to go and fetch him—'

'No, no, you were telling me about your housekeeper—Lily—she can bring him.'

'No, she's scared of flying,' Evie said. 'She told me so once. And Mark mustn't come alone. I'll go and collect him. I'll leave tomorrow and we'll be back the day after.'

The young men exclaimed over the idea of losing her,

but Hope thanked her in a way that allowed no further discussion. Justin threw her a look of gratitude.

When the meal was over Evie announced that she would retire at once, to make an early departure next morning. She would have liked to talk privately to Justin, but that could wait. This time belonged to Hope.

But later that night she had a surprise. As she was about to put out her light there came a knock on her door. It was Hope.

'I hope I don't come too late, but I had to have a brief word with you,' she said. 'We've had no chance to get to know each other, but I believe that nobody knows my son—' she lingered over the two words '—better than you.'

'I don't think that's really true,' Evie said hesitantly. 'I've known him only a few weeks.'

Hope gave an expressive shrug.

'Is time what really matters? Something tells me you know him better after a month than anyone else in a lifetime.'

'I don't believe he's let himself get close to anyone,' Evie agreed, 'except Mark.'

'Ah, yes, Mark. How I long to meet him. How generous of you to make it possible. I'll leave you now to get your sleep, and wish you a safe journey.'

She enfolded Evie in a scented embrace and departed imperiously.

Mark was waiting for her, eager to hear everything that had happened. Justin had given him part of the story and now Evie filled in with the rest.

On the flight back to Naples he kept looking at his watch.

'Counting the minutes?' she teased.

He nodded. 'Thirty minutes until we land, and thirty to get through Customs.'

'And then you'll meet your new family.'

'And you'll be there too? I mean, you're part of the family now, aren't you?'

'Well, not really.'

'But you and Dad—you know.'

'I'm not sure I do.'

'You *know*! He always used to cheer up when you wore your bikini.'

There it was again, the assumption that she and Justin were together for good. She tested the idea, wanting to know if the old alarm at commitment would start up. Instead she felt as if a smile was growing deep inside her.

As she'd expected, Justin and Hope were waiting at the airport. Hope kept her eyes on the boy as he neared her and Justin said, 'Mark, this is your grandmother.'

Mark and Evie had been practising this moment all the way on the plane and now he was ready. Gravely he offered his hand, saying, *'Buon giorno, signora.'*

Hope gave a cry of delight and was about to embrace him when she caught his eye, remembered how boys felt about being cuddled in public, and shook his hand instead, a piece of tact that won her Mark's goodwill.

While they sized each other up Justin drew Evie close, laying his cheek briefly against hers.

'Hope has been in agonies waiting for your return,' he said, adding softly, 'and so have I.'

In the car going home they were alert for Mark's needs, ready to smooth his path with this new and strange relative. But it was unnecessary. Hope and Mark were instantly on each other's wavelength and in a few minutes he was calling her Nonna, the Italian word for Grandma.

After that it was like a replay of their own arrival a few days earlier. Toni and the sons were there at the villa, this time offering a boisterous greeting that Mark seemed to enjoy. Evie could see that he was going to fit into the family even more easily than Justin.

Justin escorted her upstairs to her room and closed the door firmly behind them before taking her into his arms.

'I've missed you,' he murmured between kisses. 'Where have you been all this time?'

'All this time?' she teased him happily. 'One day?'

'You know I need you.'

'Don't tell me you've been thinking of me with all your new family to get used to. How are you getting on with your mother?'

'Well enough.'

'Well enough? Is that all you can say?'

'For the moment, yes. It's all a bit much—it'll hit me later, I dare say.'

'Yes, I suppose it's a lot to take in.'

'I know Hope is my mother. You've only got to look at us to see it. And yet—there's a part of me that doesn't believe it. I keep expecting to wake up and find that it was a dream.'

'But you won't,' she said tenderly. 'It's real. She's truly your mother, and the best part of all is that she didn't give you away. You weren't rejected. You were loved from the first moment. And you still are. That's what's so wonderful about it, that her love has been like an arc, stretching over the years from that moment to this, linking them.'

'Yes, of course,' he said. 'You put things so well. It takes me a little longer.'

'That doesn't matter. Things are coming together in their own good time. That's what counts. It's going to be all right, my darling. Everything's going to be all right.'

Later she was to wonder how she could have been so blind and stupid as not to see the pit opening at their feet. He had seen it but, in his inarticulate way, hadn't known how to tell her until it was too late.

CHAPTER TEN

THE Villa Rinucci was in turmoil. For days everything was dedicated to the great party at which Hope would introduce her new son to her friends. It would be organised along the same lines as her birthday festivities, but grander still. The whole world must know that she rejoiced in her son.

While she buried herself in menus and wine lists the two families worked at getting better acquainted. Justin spent time with Toni and Primo. His relationship with Primo was slightly edgy, but he worked hard at being cordial, conscious of what he owed him. They were both businessmen, and Primo had business interests in England, and on that level they could meet.

Francesco and Luke had left the villa to attend to their work, promising to return for the party. The twins still had a bedroom each at the villa, although both had apartments in Naples where, according to their mother, they 'got up to no good' and very much enjoyed doing so.

But for the moment their apartments were left empty as they devoted themselves to entertaining Evie and Mark. Mark gravitated instinctively to the boyish Carlo, adopting him as a favourite uncle. This was no surprise, according to his caustic twin, since Carlo had been blessed with the mind of a child.

Carlo responded in kind, and the cheerful insults flew back and forth, sometimes in English, in honour of the guests, but becoming more Italian as the atmosphere grew livelier. Mark, Evie was amused to notice, was

145

making eager notes, desperate not to lose a single rude word, while she leaned close to Justin and translated for him.

The merry battle continued for most of the evening, engulfing the entire family, until Hope called them to order through her laughter. Mark went to bed blissfully happy and spent the next day practising Neapolitan insults until Carlo frantically covered his mouth, muttering, 'I'll tell you what that means when you're older.'

'Much older,' said Evie, who was also learning fast.

Her own preference was for Ruggiero, a dark horse. He was a quiet, thoughtful young man, with a kind of subdued fierceness about him that sometimes reminded her of Justin. But the great love of his life was his motorbike and, after the first startled recognition, he and Evie greeted each other as kindred spirits.

One day they vanished for several hours so that he could demonstrate his bike. There was a brief tense moment just before they departed, when Ruggiero explained formally to Justin that he was taking Evie away for the afternoon, 'with your consent.'

'Oi!' Evie said. 'With his consent or without it. I don't need his permission. Come on.'

She gave Justin's cheek a quick kiss and hurried out, eager to try the new toy.

They were out much longer than she'd intended, finally driving up the road to the villa, exhilarated and on the best of terms, to find the whole family watching their approach from the terrace.

'You're late for supper,' Carlo yelled down. 'We've eaten it all.'

'It was delicious,' Mark cried. 'The best ever.'

'But of course we saved you some,' Hope said, smiling. 'It will be ready when you've freshened up. There is no hurry.'

The meal was, as Mark had promised, delicious. She and Ruggiero dined together while Mark helped to serve them, chattering all the time. There was no sign of Justin.

She sought him out later.

'Aren't you going to tell me about your day?' she asked.

'I think I may be able to do some business with Primo. There's a lot to discuss, but I see it happening.'

'And you'll make a pot of money?'

'Hopefully.'

'Fine. Then you've had a good day.'

'I hope you enjoyed yours.'

'It was wonderful,' she said blissfully. 'As soon as we get back to England I'm going to sell my machine and buy one like his. The speed! I've never known anything like it.'

'I was worried about you,' Justin said quietly, with the smallest vibration of anger in his voice.

'There was no need. You knew I was with Ruggiero.'

'Driving on a strange bike over strange roads. And I don't even like to think what speed you were doing.'

'Then don't,' she said briskly. That 'with your consent' still rankled. 'I can control a bike at speed.'

'Control? You mean he let you ride that thing in front?'

'In the end, yes. No way was I going to be content riding pillion.'

'You're mad.'

'You've always known that. What's so different now?'

'I was worried,' he shouted. 'Can't you understand that?'

Instantly she was contrite. She had forgotten how he took things to heart.

'Yes, I can understand,' she said gently. 'Don't worry about me. I needed that ride, but I've got the madness out of my system, at least for a while.'

'Yes, promise me that you won't do it again.'

'I will not. I'll want another ride before I leave here.'

'But not in the front. Pillion is OK, but—'

'Justin, stop there. I decide what's OK for me, not you. Now let's leave this.'

His eyes were dark and angry.

'I'm not ready to leave it. I don't like you risking your life, and I don't like you gadding off for hours with another man—'

'Another man? You mean that boy who's two years younger than I am? Nonsense. I'm like an older sister to him.'

'Did he treat you like an older sister?'

'Of course he did,' she said, trying to banish the memory of Ruggiero's arms about her body when he had been riding pillion, and the gleam of admiration in his eyes that had had nothing to do with motorbikes.

He had flirted with her in a way that had danced to the edge of acceptability, and had then danced nimbly away again when she had fended him off with laughter. It hadn't troubled her. Flirting was one of the great pleasures of her life, but she always knew when to stop.

But Justin would never be able to believe that, she realised. Perhaps it was time to give up flirtations.

'He treated me like a fellow motorbike nutter. It's a club. We're all crazy about the same thing. Plus he was entertaining me to leave you free for your mother.'

'Hope has plenty to see to. You and I could have spent the afternoon together.'

'And miss doing business with Primo? Look, I'm sorry. Let's forget about it.'

'As long as you promise not to do it again.'

Part of her wanted to agree to whatever pleased him, but another part of her simply couldn't yield to possessiveness, even his.

'I said leave it,' she said quietly.

'I suppose that's my answer.'

'No, the answer is—stop trying to give me orders. Stop trying to control me.'

He took a sharp intake of breath and she looked up to find something in his eyes that might have been fear. They stared at each other, both equally shocked by the silly quarrel that had come out of nowhere and taken them both by surprise.

Then he pulled back quickly. 'Sorry,' he said. 'I'm sorry. I don't know what came over me.'

Softened, she reached out. 'Darling—'

'Just forget it, will you?' he said hastily. Then he turned and walked away from her without a backward glance.

Evic was left feeling saddened and angry with herself that she hadn't handled it better. A noise from above made her look up to see Hope at the top of the stairs. She wasn't looking at Evie and after a moment she walked away. It was impossible to tell how much she had heard.

Then Evie forgot everything in the rush of last-minute preparations. She spent a wonderful day among the fashion shops of Naples, returning with a black silk clinging creation that gave her a dazzling new persona, quite different from the boyish biker.

In this gown she was elegant and sophisticated. She would do Justin credit.

He knocked at her door just as she was trying to decide what jewellery to wear. She owned very little as most of her money went on the bike.

But Justin had the solution, holding up a diamond pendant and diamond earrings that were perfect with the dress.

'You bought these for me?' she asked in delight.

'No, they're from Hope. She asked me to give them to you.'

It passed across her mind briefly that he always referred to his mother as Hope, but then she was distracted by the beauty of the diamonds as she fixed the earrings into place.

'She bought these for me?' she asked in wonder.

'No, I think she already had them.'

'Put the pendant on for me,' she begged, turning her back.

He fastened the clasp, then let his hands rest on her bare shoulders. They were warm and strong, giving her a good feeling.

'I'm sorry,' he said. 'I shouldn't have got mad at you for going out the other day. I know you're not quite sane where motorbikes are concerned.'

'I'll let that insult pass,' she told him, smiling. 'Anyway, it was my fault too. I was cross with Ruggiero for asking your permission to take me out, and you got the backlash. I should have remembered that he's Italian and they have more formal ideas about families.'

He dropped a kiss on the nape of her neck and she shivered with pleasure.

'I don't think you should do that when we're going

to the party in a few minutes,' she said in a shaking voice.

'No.' He sighed. 'Perhaps it's not very wise. I just wanted you to know—well, anyway. Shall we go downstairs?'

'While we still can?'

'Yes,' he growled.

From the moment they appeared Evie knew that the evening was going to be a triumphant success. The food was laid out on long, groaning tables—Neapolitan grain pie, sautéed artichokes with baby potatoes, fruits, creams, the best wines served in fine crystal.

Hope had left nothing to chance, something which, Evie was beginning to feel, was typical of her. The young girl whose baby had been brutally stolen had grown into a woman of authority, armoured, imposing her will on life.

Times had changed. The child who once had to be hidden could now be announced to the world, and she was going to glory in it.

Justin and Mark stood by her side as a hundred guests arrived, and within an hour everyone in the room knew who he was. This might be Hope's night, but it was also his.

When everyone had something to eat and drink Evie looked for Hope.

'Thank you,' she said, touching the diamonds. 'They're beautiful. Justin said that they were your own.'

'Yes. They were given to me years ago by my husband. Toni knows I have given them to you, and he agrees. We hope that soon you will be one of us.'

She floated away without giving Evie a chance to confirm or deny it. That was her way. Hope Rinucci had made her wishes known. With amusement, Evie realised that she had been not so much welcomed into the family as ordered into it.

'You look lonely,' said a voice beside her in Italian. It was Primo.

'No, I'm not lonely. I've just been talking to Hope.'

'Has my mother told you what she's planned for you?' Primo asked with a grin.

'Something like that.'

'Don't be annoyed with her, Evie. She has a kind heart and she wants everyone to be as happy as she is.'

'I know that. I'm not annoyed.'

He held out his arms. 'The music's starting. Dance with me.'

As they waltzed he said, 'You're causing a sensation tonight. No man can take his eyes off you, and they all envy Justin.'

'Stop talking nonsense,' she told him demurely.

He laughed and they danced contentedly for a while. It was true, what he had said. All eyes were on her. Men clamoured for her hand, but she sat out the next dance, talking to Primo.

Then she saw Justin coming towards them and wondered if he would ask her to dance. But something stopped him when he was near, and he turned aside to sweep a beauty into his arms.

'Primo, you must stop doing that,' Evie said.

'What am I doing?' he asked innocently.

'Talking to me in Italian. That's what puts Justin off. It excludes him, you know that.'

His shrug was expressive. 'Excludes? Do you think he feels excluded now that he has been included in so much that he never had before? He's the hero of the hour.'

She stared. 'You dislike him, don't you?'

'Why are you surprised? He's not a man who's easy to like.'

'I suppose it's—all this talk about brothers.'

'But we're not brothers. There's no blood tie between us at all. He is my mother's son—and I am not.'

The touch of bitterness in his voice was like a blindfold being torn from her eyes.

'You're jealous,' she said incredulously.

'Of course I am. Why not? Because I'm a grown man and you think such feelings are only for children?'

'I suppose I meant something like that,' she said wryly. 'But it's nonsense, of course. There's always a small part of the child that never entirely grows up. It stays with the adult like a little ghost, haunting him and colouring all his thoughts and feelings.'

After a moment Primo nodded and said in a more sympathetic voice, 'I see. Him too.'

'Naturally. What do you think it was like for him, thinking himself unwanted by two mothers? You've nothing to feel jealous about.'

'I'm surprised at you, Evie. You of all people should understand Italians better, for I consider myself Italian despite my English father. We're not like the cold-blooded Anglo-Saxons. For us the family is still the centre of everything, and the mother is the centre of the family. That was true in the past, it is true now, and it always will be.

'Hope has been the only mother I ever knew. In my childhood we were exceptionally close. For years I regarded myself as her eldest son. Then I discovered that I wasn't. I began to wonder if our closeness had been an illusion. Was I no more than a stopgap for the son she'd lost?'

Evie made a sudden gesture. His words were so uncannily reminiscent of what Justin had said of his own adoptive parents.

'But it was you who found him,' Evie reminded Primo. 'You've searched for years.'

'For her sake. I wanted her to be happy. Now she is, and I am glad. But also—' he gave a sheepish smile '— I am jealous.'

'But you won't let it spoil things, will you?' she pleaded.

'Of course not. Despite what I said before, he is my brother. But who says that brothers have to agree all the time?'

She slipped away from him, brooding on his words and trying to ignore a little voice in her head that said something was wrong. On the surface all was well, with Justin, as Primo had said, 'the hero of the hour'.

And yet, she thought, troubled, and yet—

'Is it my turn now?'

She turned and saw Justin.

'I haven't been able to get near you all evening,' he said wryly.

'I could say the same about you,' she teased. 'I must be the only woman you haven't danced with.'

'And the only woman I want to dance with.'

He opened his arms and she went into them.

'I'm so happy for you,' she said. 'Who could ever have believed that it would all turn out as well as this? It's a dream come true.'

'More than that,' he said. 'How could I ever have imagined this?'

'Never,' she said happily. 'It just shows, you never know what's around the corner.'

He held her a little closer and she let her head fall on his shoulder, while the music played, soft and low. She thought back, just a few weeks, to before she had known this man. Now there was nowhere she wanted to be but in his arms.

She looked up, expecting to see him sharing her delight, but what she saw in his face startled her.

Instead of pleasure and satisfaction there was only confusion and a kind of bafflement. With a sense of alarm, she realised that she had never seen a man look so desperate.

'Must you go?' Hope pleaded the next day. 'Have I only recovered my son to lose him again so soon?'

'You won't lose me,' Justin said. 'I'll be back, but I must attend to my business.'

'Please, Dad,' Mark begged. 'Just a few more days? It's great here. Evie wants to stay too, don't you?'

Smiling, she shook her head. 'I have to get back to England too, but perhaps—' A thought had come to her, seductive in its promise of pleasure and joy.

She exchanged a silent look with Hope, who understood her at once and beamed.

'At least let Mark stay a little longer,' she said. 'Then I can be sure you will come back.'

Mark gave his father a beseeching look and Justin nodded.

'Of course,' he said. 'If that's what he'd like.'

Mark began a war dance of delight and his uncles Carlo and Ruggiero joined in. Justin relaxed and nodded.

'I'll come for him in September,' he said.

'And you will bring Evie with you?' Hope urged. 'And then we can discuss your marriage. Perhaps we can even have it here.'

'We can talk about that later, Mamma,' Justin said quickly.

'Of course, my son. I understand. I'm a steamroller, aren't I? I make plans for everyone and I don't let anyone else get a word in. It's just that I'm so anxious to welcome Evie into the family.'

Warmly she kissed Evie's cheek.

'My first daughter-in-law. How glad I will be to have you—'

'Mamma,' Primo murmured, 'you're doing it again.'

Everyone laughed heartily, except Justin, who gave only a faint smile. His mind seemed to be elsewhere. Evie was too preoccupied with thoughts of the coming blissful time, alone with him, to find this ominous.

Everyone came to see them off at the airport. Hope kissed her and whispered, 'Soon, my dear daughter.'

'I called Tom and told him to meet the flight,' Justin said when they were in the air. Tom was his driver.

'Will he take me to my apartment, or shall I call a taxi?'

'Don't be ridiculous,' he said, almost angrily. 'You're coming home with me. That is—' he became uneasy '— if you want to.'

She laughed. 'I just wanted to know what you had in mind.'

'I need to be alone with you. I haven't had that for days.'

She nodded vigorously.

It was late when they reached home. Lily opened the door, smiling to see Evie. Acting on instructions, she'd prepared a room for her and showed her up to it, followed by Justin.

'I've made a cold supper for you,' she said when Evie's bags were deposited in the bedroom, 'and it's on the table downstairs. Now, if it's all right, I'm going to bed.'

'Goodnight,' they both said.

The moment the door closed behind her they were in each other's arms, eager to make love and rediscover each other. He drew her down on to the bed, kissing her urgently as he removed her clothes and she removed his. And for a while it was as though the last week had never happened and everything was as it had been.

The sleep afterwards was deep and blissful. She awoke to the guilty thought that they hadn't eaten the supper after all and turned her head to share the joke with Justin.

He wasn't beside her on the bed, but by the window. He was naked, standing with his eyes fixed on her, so still that he might have been a statue. And the air was jagged.

'Justin, what is it?' she whispered. 'What's wrong?'

'I don't know. I woke up in a black cloud. It came over me while I was asleep, but it's as though I've been waiting for it. It was bound to happen.'

'So, you've got a touch of depression, but you're tired and you've had a lot of stuff to deal with. It'll pass.'

'I wish I believed that. But ever since I met my mother I've waited for the right feelings to come. At the party I looked around at them, my whole family, the features that so many of us share, and I kept saying to myself, *I've come home. This is it, the happy ending where I finally know who I am and where I belong.*

'And Evie, do you know what happened? Nothing. I repeated it again and again, waiting for the spring of joy that would make everything as it should be. But there's nothing there.'

'But my love, of course there isn't. It's much too soon. Only fairy tales give you an instant happy ending.

In life it takes longer. You haven't lived all these years in a vacuum. You've become a certain kind of person—'

'Harsh, suspicious, unfeeling—'

'Don't say that about yourself. You're not unfeeling, and I know that better than anyone. If anything you're hurt too easily, so you've tried to make yourself unfeeling, but it hasn't worked.'

'Don't you think I'd know more about that than you?' he asked quietly.

'No, I don't. You're the man I love and I'm going to go on loving. I know it won't be easy, but whatever demons you've got in your head I'll drive them away.'

'I wish I thought you could, that anyone could. I shouldn't have brought you home here with me, I shouldn't have made love to you. Forgive me for that. My only excuse is that I couldn't have borne not to. I had to be close to you again, and then to talk to you like this and tell you what's becoming clear to me, although God knows I don't want to face it.'

'What?' she asked, trying to quell the rising alarm in her. 'What is it that you don't want to face?'

'That we can't love each other and it's better if we say goodbye while there's still time.'

CHAPTER ELEVEN

THROUGH her shock Evie realised that this had always been coming. Underlying the joy at Naples, there had been something wrong. She'd sensed it without understanding, or perhaps not letting herself understand. Nor would she face it now. He was her life and she wouldn't give up without a fight.

'Who says we can't love each other?' she asked angrily. 'You?'

'What I *am* says it, and what I am can't be changed.' He gave a wry, mirthless smile. 'Oddly enough, you were the one who showed me that.'

'I did? How? When?'

'When you came back after that day with Ruggiero and I tried to stop you doing it again. You told me not to give you orders or try to control you. Do you remember?'

'Yes. And then you had such a strange look on your face—as though I'd said something terrible.'

'You had. You'd said exactly what Margaret used to say to me when we were married. I was possessive and controlling—'

'But that's only because you were afraid of losing her, because you'd lost everyone else. Surely you realise that?'

'Yes, of course. I did even then. But knowing why you're behaving intolerably doesn't mean you can stop yourself. I knew I was driving her further away from me every day. And I still couldn't stop.

159

'I saw her start to hate me and it made me worse. The more her love died the more I tried to force it back, and of course I failed because no woman can love a monster and tyrant for very long.'

'Don't say that about yourself,' she cried passionately.

'It's the truth. I know what I am and I can't be anything else.'

'You can,' she said stubbornly, 'because now you'll have me.'

He came forward in the faint light and stood beside her where she was sitting on the bed. She felt his warmth and breathed in the thrilling spicy scent of him as he put his hands on each side of her face, gazing down at her.

'I've told myself that,' he whispered, 'a thousand times when I've been trying to believe that I had every right to bind you to me. But I've always known that I have no right at all.

'Once I started thinking about Margaret I began remembering other things, how much I loved her at first, so much that it frightened me. But that didn't stop me turning into—what I became, what I still am. I destroyed Margaret and sent her off to her death. I won't risk doing that to you.'

She answered by reaching up, running her hands over his naked body and pulling him down beside her.

'Stop talking so much,' she said fiercely. 'It's all words. They don't matter. I know there are problems but we can beat them—like this—and this—'

She was kissing him as she spoke, speaking to him on the deeper level where they could find each other. But even as she did so she knew that this wasn't the way to convince him. She possessed his heart and his body, but his mind was fighting her. Without all three, he could never be truly hers.

As if reading her thoughts, he gave a convulsive jerk and pulled himself free.

'Evie, don't, please—'

'You can't destroy me,' she said passionately. 'I'm strong.'

'Yes. Strong enough to fight me, and fight me with the most devilish weapons, because you know the ones I find hardest to resist. But is that the love either of us wants? *She* fought me. In the end we did nothing else but fight, and I think—' his voice shook, as though the next words tore him apart '—I think, at last, I was actually trying to drive her away.'

'But why?'

'Because I learned to do that, long ago. Life's less painful if I'm the one who's doing the rejecting. I told you I was a coward at heart. Accept it.'

'I won't accept it because it isn't true. A coward could never have made the journey that you did to find out about your mother.'

'But it was your journey, that I took because you made me. Without you I'd have shut myself away in my steel trap. Let me tell you about that trap, because you need to know about it, and fear it. I was living there when we met. It's a small place, because that way I can guard every inch. It has two barred windows, but they're small too because it's easier to keep out the world that way.'

'Don't,' she cried in agony, putting her hands over her ears.

But he pulled them away and kept a firm grip on her wrists.

'You've got to know,' he said harshly. 'You've got to understand what I have to do.'

'I don't want to hear any more about that cage. We broke it open and we're taking it to pieces.'

'Once I thought so. If you only knew how I hoped for that, because you could break it open if anyone could. But you can't. Not even you.'

'I don't believe you're giving up on us that easily,' she cried.

'Because you don't know what I'm really like, the shadows inside me that I can't get rid of, not even now. That's why I have to make the decision for both of us, but don't ever call it easy.' He looked at her out of haggard eyes. 'Forgive me, Evie. Try to forgive me.'

'I won't forgive you,' she flashed. 'We've been given such a precious gift, and you're throwing it away.'

'Because the man I've grown into can't do anything else. Don't you see? That's the cage, and that's why it'll never be destroyed. I have to live in it, because for me there's no longer any choice. But I'm damned if I'll imprison you in there with me.'

'And what about Mark?'

'Mark's found what he needs with his new family. You did that for him, and I'll always be grateful.'

'And I'm supposed to just shrug my shoulders and go away, leaving you to shrivel?'

'You deserve better than to live in a cage.'

'Don't you?'

'It's a safe place. There's no feeling there.'

'Don't try to tell me you're unfeeling,' she raged help-lessly. 'I know better.'

'You think you do.'

'Do you think a woman doesn't know if a man loves her when she's with him, when they lie together? I've seen your eyes and heard you whisper my name. You can't shut out those times or pretend they didn't happen. They were wonderful.'

'They were very enjoyable,' he said harshly. 'We're good in bed together. Nobody could deny that, but let's not get sentimental about it.'

His voice fell cruelly on her ears, leaving her too shocked to speak.

'You really fight dirty,' she whispered.

'Have you only just discovered that? Well, it's time you found out, and you're better off knowing the worst of me.'

'Stop trying to frighten me.'

'If you're not frightened, you ought to be. Go away from me, Evie. I just hurt everyone I touch. I can't help it. I wish we'd met years ago, but now it's too late for me. Can't you understand that?'

'No, and I won't believe it,' she flashed.

'What can't you believe? That I can plan to leave you at the same time as doing this?'

He pulled her hard against him, cradling her head for the most crushing kiss he'd ever given her. She returned it in full, driven as desperately as he. Like him she had something to prove, and she tried to prove it by more than meeting him halfway. Where he had been tender before, now he made love fiercely, but she contended with him in ferocity.

Only a few minutes ago she'd told herself that to unite with him physically but not mentally would be useless. Now she abandoned all thoughts of his mind. This might be her last chance, and she would win the game in any way she could.

And victory felt in her grasp with every fevered caress. He had said he couldn't do 'three little words', but he could love her with power and abandon, revealing the depths of his need with every movement. Her answering love was a promise from her soul. He must sense it and answer it. He *must*.

But in the last moments she felt her victory slipping away. It was over. He had loved her tonight as never before and, in that mood, he would sever himself from her for ever. She sensed that through her skin, her heartbeat.

When at last they lay in each other's arms she felt his face against her skin and knew that he was weeping.

Then she wept with him.

Evie told herself that she had been here before. A relationship that had looked promising came to an end and she was once more a free agent. There was sadness but there was also relief at her escape.

That was then. This was now.

In the past she had always been the one to call a halt, fearing for her liberty. This time it was like being tossed into a black pit.

She had loved Justin with an intensity of feeling that she'd never known before, giving herself to him, body, heart and soul, with a completeness that had surprised even herself. To love and be with him always had become more important than anything in life, even liberty.

Sometimes she could work herself up into hating him, reminding herself of his cruel words about getting sentimental, telling herself that he'd meant every one. If she worked hard, she could almost believe it.

At other times she was haunted by the conviction that he'd been forcing himself to say what would drive her away, not for his own sake, but for hers. That belief was the worst pain of all, because it meant that he'd chosen to withdraw into the bleak cage where no sun shone and where her love couldn't reach him. And he'd done it for her.

Before leaving his house she had returned to Justin the diamonds that Hope had given her.

'She meant these for her daughter-in-law,' she said. 'So I can't keep them.'

She was gone before Mark returned. The boy sent her emails, demanding to know when she was coming back, refusing to believe that everything was over. She could hardly believe it herself.

She wrote back, carefully explaining that she and Justin had decided that they had no future together, but that she would always like to hear from him.

He emailed her regularly. Sometimes he would add news about his father, who was apparently snowed under in work. There was never anything personal, except that he sometimes added, *Dad says hallo.*

She wrote to Hope, thanking her for her welcome, and the way she had underlined it with the diamonds.

> *I cannot keep them. But it will always make me happy to remember them.*

Hope replied in a furious temper.

> *You've both taken leave of your senses. I don't want diamonds. I want the daughter-in-law that I love. I want a wedding and more grandchildren (not necessarily in that order. I'm not a prude.) I shall keep the jewels locked away until you both see reason.*

Evie had to smile at that, recognising the loyalty and affection that lay beneath Hope's words, as well as the annoyance that the world was daring to disobey her.

The weather turned colder. Mark wrote to say that they were going to Naples for Christmas.

She could have spent her own Christmas with Debra and her family, but she made an excuse. The sight of Debra's husband and children was more than she could have borne just now.

She spent the festive season locked in her apartment working until she was exhausted, and remembering the words Debra had once uttered.

'One day I hope you'll fall hook, line and sinker for a man you can't have. It'll be a new experience for you.'

Her friend had been joking, but it wasn't funny any more.

When the doorbell rang on a freezing February day Evie didn't know who to expect.

'*Mark!*'

'Can I come in?'

'Of course.' She stood back and ushered him inside, glancing into the corridor outside. But Justin wasn't there and she forced back the brief surge of hope.

How quickly children grew! Mark had changed, even in six months. The young man he would soon be was starting to show in his face. He was also taller, as she realised when he hugged her.

She was longing to ask him a million questions—about himself, about his father and their life together. But she held off until he was sitting in her tiny kitchen, tucking into a hastily prepared snack.

'I'm glad to see your appetite is as healthy as ever,' she said. 'Another piece of apple crumble?'

He nodded, his mouth still full, and she loaded his plate again.

'How did you know my address?' she asked.

'You wrote it on the outside of the packet when you sent my memory stick back that time.'

'But that was ages ago. You made a note of it then?'

'We agreed to keep in touch.'

'Yes, we did. You really are your father's son, aren't you? He's ultra-methodical too.'

Merely talking about Justin was a pleasure. She forced herself to relinquish it. It was too dangerously sweet.

'So tell me,' she said, 'what's been happening. How was Christmas?'

'Great. Nonna's ever so nice, but I wish you'd been there. I wished it all the time. I kept thinking you might turn up as a surprise, but you didn't.'

'Mark, dear, it isn't possible. Your father and I aren't together any more.'

'But you could be,' he pleaded.

'No. It was never going to work out. I'm out of his life now, for good.'

'But I don't want you to be out of mine,' he said stubbornly. 'That's why I'm here. I want you to come to the funeral.'

'Whose funeral?'

'Mum's. He brought her home. He started talking to me one day, about Mum, and how I felt about her still being in Switzerland. I said I'd like to have her here, so he arranged for her to be flown back and reburied in that churchyard you saw.'

'That's wonderful,' she said. 'It's what you wanted, isn't it?'

He nodded, his eyes bright. 'I always wanted to have her home, but he didn't think it mattered, and I couldn't explain. But he's different now, Evie. He understands things he didn't understand before.'

She was silent, feeling a glow inside her that she had

thought never to know again. It was almost like happiness. For she knew, as surely as if Justin were standing there beside her, that she was responsible for this.

She had thought their love had turned into a barren thing, but if he'd learned the way to reach out to his son then some good had come from it.

He understands things he didn't understand before.

She could keep that and treasure it.

'The funeral's the day after tomorrow,' Mark said. 'Will you come?'

She gasped. 'Mark, I can't. I really can't.'

'But you must, because it's down to you, isn't it?'

'I may have said something to him once, but—no, it was his decision.'

'But you made him do it.'

She shook her head. 'Nobody makes him do anything.'

'You do. He did listen to you, although he pretended not to.'

She tried to deny it, but it was hard when he was saying what she longed to hear.

'Anyway,' she said, 'I expect your mother's family will be there. They might not like my being there.'

'She didn't have anyone. It'll just be Dad and me—and you.'

She was shocked by how badly she wanted to say yes. Just to see Justin again, speak to him, watch his face. All these things would be wonderful and terrible.

Then Mark stunned her again by remarking, 'He's still got your picture.'

'What picture?'

'One of the two I took of you that night you came to the house. Dad cropped it down to your head and printed it out small.'

'You saw him?'

His smile called her naïve. ''Course not. But he forgot to wipe it off my computer afterwards. So I checked his wallet, and it was there last week.'

'Mark, you shouldn't have looked in his wallet.'

'But I had to,' he said with an air of injured innocence. 'How can I find things out if I don't check the facts?'

'Don't you try to blind me with science, my lad,' she said, half laughing, half crying.

It was madness to feel suddenly full of joy. He'd kept her picture. Better still, he'd listened to her. In a way they were still part of each other's lives, even if they never met again.

'Mark, did you tell him you were coming here?'

The boy shook his head. Before she could speak, his mobile phone rang.

'Hallo, Dad. It's all right, I haven't disappeared. I came to see Evie. Dad? Are you there? I'm at Evie's apartment. I told her about Mum and asked her to come to the funeral, but she says she can't.'

'Let me talk to him,' she said, holding out her hand for the phone. 'Justin?'

'Yes,' came his voice after a moment, and even that one word, tinny and distorted as it was, had the power to move her.

'I just want you to know that Mark is quite safe. He'll be on his way home in a few minutes. Please don't worry.'

'I don't worry if he's with you, but I'm sorry he troubled you.'

'He's no trouble. And Justin—I'm glad—about his mother—'

'It was what he badly wanted. I should have seen that at the start. He says he's told you his idea.'

'For me to come to the funeral, yes, but it doesn't seem right.'

She stopped, hardly daring to let herself think further ahead.

Then he said, 'He wants it badly, but of course I'll understand if—I couldn't really expect you—'

'I'll come, of course I will. I didn't think you'd want to see me there.'

Silence. She wished she knew what she could read into it.

'Mark misses you,' he said at last. 'I think it would mean a lot to him.'

Say that you miss me, she thought wistfully.

Silence.

'Then I'll come.'

'I'll send my driver to collect him. Thank you for looking after him today. Goodnight.'

'Goodnight,' she said, trying to match his formal tone although it hurt her that they should have to be polite, like strangers.

'You're coming?' said Mark, who'd been listening. 'That's great.'

'Yes, I'll be there.'

'Did Dad sound angry?'

'No, he wasn't angry, he was just—he wasn't anything.' That was the only way, she realised, to describe the sense of blankness that had reached her down the phone.

But telephones made everything different. It would be all right when she saw him.

'While we wait,' she said cheerfully, 'why don't you tell me some more about Christmas? Did you find it a bit quiet, because Italians don't really celebrate Christmas. They wait until Epiphany on January 6th.'

'Yes, but Nonna said 'cos I was English I must have presents at Christmas, like always. And then, when it was Epiphany, she said I must have more presents because that's what everyone did. I tried to say I didn't expect two lots of presents, but Nonna told me I'd just have to put up with it.'

'I can just hear Hope saying that,' Evie mused, relishing the picture.

'And I learned lots of Neapolitan words. I remembered them for you.'

They chatted in this way until the bell rang, announcing Justin's driver. He said he would call for her again to take her to the funeral in two days' time, and bring her home afterwards.

When Mark had gone she plunged into her work and tried to think of nothing else. But pages passed before her eyes, making no impact. In the end she took the motorbike and rode at speed for hours until she no longer knew where she was. Which pretty much described her whole life, she thought.

For once the speed didn't bring the usual sense of release. She knew now that she was fleeing something that would always lie in wait, just ahead.

When the day came she chose an austere dark blue suit, and checked her appearance again and again. She was trying to stay calm, knowing that soon she would meet Justin again for the first time in months. And he would look different to her, because now she knew that he kept her picture with him all the time.

She wouldn't let herself think of what might happen then. That way lay madness. But, despite her good resolutions, the thought of seeing him after the long lonely months, studying his face, the way he smiled at her, all these made her heart beat faster.

Finally the cemetery came into view and at once her mind began to replay her last visit, in early summer when the leaves were green and the sun was high. Now it was the depth of winter—cold, wet, and miserable.

Mark came to meet her at the church door, taking her by the hand.

'Thank you,' he whispered. 'We're all ready.'

She was startled by the bleakness she found inside. As Mark had said, there was only himself and his father, with no family on his mother's side. Justin was standing in the front row with his back to her. He turned as she approached, and at first she didn't recognise him.

He was older and thinner, but that wasn't the worst of it. His face now had the hard, withered look that she'd feared to see.

'Hallo,' she greeted him softly.

He seemed to take a moment to respond, as though not quite sure where he was. Then he inclined his head a little towards her.

'Thank you for coming,' he said politely. 'It was important to Mark.'

'I'm glad he wanted me.'

The priest appeared, wanting to know if they were ready to begin. Justin nodded and glanced at Mark, who went to stand beside him, taking Evie's hand in his so that she was on his other side.

It was a short service. There was very little to be done. Justin kept his eyes fixed on the flower-covered coffin. Watching him, Evie remembered what he had told her about Margaret, how much he had loved her, and how it had all turned to hate.

What was he thinking now? Was Margaret there in

his heart again at this moment? Was there any room left for herself?

They moved outside to where the grave had been dug. Now she could see more clearly the flowers on the coffin—two bouquets of roses. One bore a card in Mark's childish hand.

To Mummy, with love always.

The card on the other was from Justin. It said simply, *Thank you.*

When the graveside rites were concluded Mark squeezed her hand, as if to say that everything was all right now. Evie looked at him, touched by the way he was reaching out to her, even at this moment.

Justin's face was like a rock, revealing nothing.

Everything was unreal. How could she be here with him, her heart alive to him as though the lonely separation had never been? As the service concluded, she saw him look at her. She went to stand in front of him, daring him not to face her.

'Are you really glad I came?' she asked. 'Not just for Mark's sake?'

He took a long time to answer and a chill crept through her.

'Yes, I'm really glad to see you,' he said at last. 'I've wondered how things were with you.'

'And I've wondered about you, whether you were well, how life was treating you.'

'It's treating me fine, as you can see.'

No, I can't see that. I can only see that your face is tense and weary, as it was when we first met.

'Do you see much of your family?'

'We have a standing invitation to Naples. Mark can go more often than I can, but Hope and I get on well.'

I thought I'd banished that defensive look from your eyes, but it's there again, and perhaps it always will be.

'I'm glad of that,' she said firmly.

'You did that for me, and I'll never forget it.'

No, in the end there was nothing I could do for you, my love.

'What about you? Have you been back to Italy?' he asked desperately.

'There hasn't been time. I've been swamped in work.'

'Well—I'm glad your career's going well.'

'Yes, very well, thank you.'

I'm grabbing all the work I can find. It fills the hours.

She'd been deluding herself with false hopes about this meeting. He hadn't wanted to see her, and now he was struggling for something to say.

'The driver will take you back as soon as you're ready,' he said. 'I hope we haven't taken up too much of your valuable time.'

There was an ache in her throat. Through the worst moments she'd clung to the hope that one day they would meet again.

But this was the meeting, and now she knew they were really at the end of the road.

When at last she could speak, she forced out words that were as formal and ugly as his own.

'Well, it's time I was going,' she said briskly. 'It's so nice to have seen you again. The best of luck.'

He drew a sharp breath and for a moment his face was constricted with pain.

'Evie,' he said harshly, 'are you all right?'

'No. You?'

He shook his head. But he would not yield.

'Goodbye,' he whispered.

She touched his cheek gently.

'Goodbye, my love,' she said. 'Goodbye.'

CHAPTER TWELVE

SHE began to lose track of time. Day seemed to follow day with little difference between them. Sometimes she felt as though she'd been translating the same book for ever and it was almost a surprise to receive three sets of galleys to check. At some time recently she must have worked on these books, but it felt like another life.

She sat at her screen for hours, crawling into bed at the last moment, getting up with the dawn, drinking black coffee before forcing herself awake with a cold shower.

Then it was back to work. Don't think. Don't listen to the phone that never rings. Don't wonder how you'll endure the rest of your life.

Mark still corresponded with her. She knew how often he went to Naples, and also how often Justin left him with his grandmother while he went away on business. She formed a vague idea that he was burying himself in work to avoid thinking and feeling, like herself.

She always worded her own emails carefully, in case Justin should see them. She couldn't bear to think of him knowing how she still pined for him when he had destroyed their love so decisively, although Mark ended every email with a hopeful, *Dad isn't dating anyone else.*

In spring she went down to the cottage. She'd been avoiding it, using the cold weather as an excuse. The truth was that she couldn't bear the thought of returning to the place where she had been with Justin, and had learned to love him.

But with the extra money he'd paid her from the sale she could do many necessary repairs, and at last the moment had to be faced. She bought a small car and drove down to Penzance.

The cottage was chilly and the emptiness felt more bleak even than she'd anticipated. There was the little kitchen where he'd cooked, and she'd begun to realise he had more facets than she'd imagined. There was the sofa where she'd awoken to find him kneeling beside her, regarding her with tender concern.

Her footsteps echoed on the flagstones, then up the stairs to the silent, empty bedrooms. She wondered how she could ever bear to be here again, but then she knew she couldn't bear to leave. This was the place where they had loved, and he would be with her here for ever.

She began to go swimming. The water was still chilly, but she found it bracing and would swim out a long way. The journey back would tire her, and that way she could get some sleep.

One morning she went out early and swam further than usual. At last she realised that it would be wise to turn back. She returned slowly, feeling the strength draining away from her while the shore seemed to recede instead of growing closer. Her arms and legs were heavy and she seemed to make no progress.

Her mind was growing fuzzy. It would be so easy to let herself fall asleep now.

Once before she'd come out this far and Justin had been alarmed, calling her back to safety, powering through the water to reach her. To tease him she had pushed on further, daring him to catch up.

That had been in the early days, before Andrew's defection, and everything had been a game, but when he'd been about to catch her she'd suddenly become very conscious of her near nakedness in the bikini, the way he was bound to seize her around the waist and draw her against him.

But he'd only grabbed her wrist and yelled something about showing a little common sense. She'd started to laugh, and he'd said, 'Hold on to me while we go back.'

She'd laughed harder, saying, 'Who needs to?' Then she had broken away from him and swam off, freshly invigorated by the sudden pounding of her blood.

She closed her eyes, reliving the moment, wondering why she hadn't seen the truth then. And would it have made any difference to the end?

'*Eee—viee!*'

The voice came from the sky, from the sea, from the air. It was all around her.

'*Eee—viee!*'

The sound narrowed down to a point on the shore. A tall, elegant woman stood there, calling and waving to her.

It was Hope.

Evie blinked, trying to realise that the impossible was happening. Somehow she brought her limbs back to life and began to make her way to shore.

As she reached shallow water and rose to her feet she stumbled, discovering just how exhausted she was. Without hesitation Hope began to wade in, oblivious to the damage to her couture clothes. Reaching Evie, she pulled her arm about her shoulders and supported her back to safety.

There, Evie could do no more than collapse on the

sand, looking up at Hope as she leaned over her, saying in a voice of total exasperation, 'Honestly, you're as bad as he is!'

Later, in the warmth of the cottage, when Evie had showered and dressed, Hope said firmly, 'Sit down and eat.'

Attired in Evie's towel dressing gown while her own clothes dried out, she had taken over the kitchen and concocted a delicious meal from whatever she'd found there. Eating it with relish, Evie recognised the hand of a genuine born home-maker.

This had always been inevitable, she realised. Part of her had known that Hope would never leave matters as they were.

'Are you angry that I came?' Hope asked, sitting at the table with her and pouring a cup of strong tea.

'Of course not. I'm glad to see you. But I thought you were in Italy, with Mark.'

'My grandson does not need me at the moment. He has the whole family to make a fuss of him. I came to England to see my son. He's the one who needs me now. You also.'

Evie gave a brief laugh. 'Oh, I'm managing.'

'Are you?' Hope asked, regarding her critically. 'It didn't seem that way out there.'

'I was just tired, getting my second wind before I swam back.'

'Perhaps, but something tells me that you were thinking dangerous thoughts.'

Before Hope's shrewd but kindly gaze Evie found that it was impossible to dissemble.

'Well, if I was, it was only for a moment,' she said. 'I'd have pulled myself together.'

'Of course. You are a woman. Somehow we always

pull ourselves together. But them—' She shrugged, dismissing and disrespecting the entire world of men.

She glanced around the cottage, taking in Evie's desk, the open books, the signs of relentless work. Watching her, Evie had the feeling that she understood everything.

'Do you ever sleep?' Hope asked at last.

'Only when I have to,' Evie admitted. 'For the rest of the time—' She shrugged.

'There is always work,' Hope agreed. 'It is as I thought. You cope better than he does.'

'You've seen him?' Evie asked eagerly. 'How is he?'

'I was with him yesterday. He's like you, working too hard, late into the night. His telephone rings constantly. He barks out his orders.' She gave a sigh. 'It is terrible.'

'We each cope in our own way,' Evie said.

'He isn't coping,' Hope said at once. 'He thinks he is, but actually he's dying. The outer shell is the same but inside he's crumbling to dust.'

'Don't,' she whispered. 'Please don't say any more.'

'But I have to. How else can I help my son? Evie, I've come to tell you that you must return to him. You *must*. Or he is finished.'

'But Hope, I didn't leave him. He sent me away. That was what he wanted.'

'Don't be ridiculous; of course that wasn't what he wanted. It's what he felt he had to do, for your sake. It was his idea of being strong, and of course he got it all wrong. He needs you. He can't survive without you.'

'He thinks he can.'

'Then you must show him his mistake. You must return to him, whether he agrees or not. If he protests, ignore him. Move in and refuse to budge. Evie, I beg you to listen to me. You're his last chance. I've never been able to do anything for my son before, but I must do this for him.'

Evie was silent, torn by temptation. The yearning for Justin was a cruel ache that pervaded her and reduced the rest of her life to rubble. And yet—

'I can't,' she said desperately. 'It isn't that I don't want to. I do. I want him so much, night and day, all the time, every minute, if you only knew—'

'You think I don't know that longing?' Hope asked wryly.

Evie had put her hands up to her head, almost tearing her hair, but at this she lowered them again.

'Yes, I suppose you do,' she said.

'When I was fifteen I fell in love with a boy a few years older. His name was Philip. He was wild and handsome and all the girls wanted him. My mother warned me against him. She said he was a bad lot. He came from a family of criminals and was just like them.

'But I didn't care. I was honoured that he chose me. I gave him whatever he wanted, sure that our love would last for ever. Of course, when I became pregnant, he didn't want to know. That was when I discovered how many other girls he had. Soon after that he was sent to prison.

'In those days unmarried mothers didn't have the help they have now. I longed to keep my baby, for I still loved Philip. I fantasised about going to see him in prison, taking our child with me. He would be so moved by the sight that he would love me again, and when he came out we would be together. Ah, the tales one tells oneself at fifteen!'

She sighed and fell silent. Evie put her hand over the older woman's and received a squeeze in return. They sat like that for a moment.

'Then my baby was born,' Hope resumed at last, 'but I never saw him. They said he'd been born dead and taken away at once. From that moment I grieved for him, and when I learned the truth it only made the grief greater, to think that he was alive somewhere and I might never see him.

'I did Jack Cayman a great disservice by marrying him without truly loving him. He had a son, Primo, and I think I tried to replace one son with another. Primo and I grew close, then Jack and I adopted another son, Luke. But you can't use one child to replace another.

'I tried to be a good mother to them, but then I met Franco and we fell in love. He was married. We couldn't be together, but Francesco was born from our love.'

'And Toni?' Evie asked shyly.

Hope gave a warm smile.

'Toni was the love of my maturity, and he still is. He always will be.'

But she did not say that Toni was the love of her life, Evie noted.

'When you both came to Naples last year,' Hope resumed, 'I was overjoyed. I looked forward to long talks with my son. I would tell him everything, and we would be united as mother and son. But—' She sighed and gave a helpless shrug.

'You didn't tell him anything?' Evie asked.

'Oh, yes, but only the bare facts. Of course, the child I'd dreamed of didn't exist. In his place was a man who'd turned himself to iron in order to endure what life had done to him. How could I share my thoughts and feelings? They would simply have embarrassed him.

'We spent long hours together talking about nothing of importance. At the end of it our hearts were still closed to each other, and I think now that his heart will remain closed, except to his son, and to you.

'He doesn't *feel* that I am his mother. He knows it with his head, but it's a meaningless word because he's never had a mother's love or care from me. That's why he always calls me Hope, never Mother.'

'Yes, I wondered about that.'

'Now I'm trying to do the only thing I can for him. He told me how he forced your parting, and why, and he's right in many ways. He *is* a dark man inside, and not every woman could cope with him. But I believe you can, and I'm here to beg you to go back and give him another chance.'

'But Hope—'

The older woman seized both her hands and spoke fiercely.

'I haven't been a good woman, Evie. I have been cruel and selfish and I've hurt many people along the way. I try to make up for it, but some things can never be put right. I've learned a great deal about men—perhaps too much.

'Some men are made to be husbands, and some to be lovers. I've known both kinds, and loved both kinds. A wise woman can sense the difference—' she gave a rueful smile '—but I was not always wise.'

'I think you're the wisest woman I know.'

'If so, I've bought that wisdom through hard and painful lessons. I told you I knew the yearning you are feeling—just for one man, because he's the only one who will do. I know when you should run from it because it will destroy you. And I know when you should listen to it. I tell you, this time you should listen. Because otherwise you will never be free.'

'How can I go back to him against his will? Maybe he secretly wanted a way out?'

'You wouldn't say that if you could see him now. If the two of you lose each other finally, you will survive, but I'm not sure that he will. He's strong in his way, but it's not the right way to help him now. You are connected to life in a way that he isn't.'

'If only I knew what was the right thing to do.'

'Listen to your heart. It will tell you all you need to know. It won't be easy for you. He's always going to be a troubled man, but he needs you desperately. And you'll have all his love, even if he finds it hard to tell you.'

Evie drew a sharp breath. 'I'll get dressed as fast as I can.'

Outside stood Justin's car and driver, both of which, Evie guessed, Hope had simply commandeered.

As they drove back to London Evie reflected, with wonder, on a lifetime spent avoiding commitment. Now she was plunging into a commitment so deep it was terrifying. But not as terrifying as a life spent without him.

When, hours later, they reached Justin's house, Hope let herself in with a key that perhaps she had also commandeered. Everywhere was very quiet, and at first Evie thought the place was empty. But then she saw him in the big garden, far away under the trees, in the fading light. She began to run.

When he looked up and saw her hurrying towards him, he grew very still. She half expected him to turn away, rejecting her, but at the last moment he opened his arms. When she went into them, they closed about her in a fierce grip.

But still he said, 'Go away, Evie. Don't do this,' while his arms held her tighter and tighter.

'Shut up,' she said. 'No more of your words. You won't get rid of me with words again. I'm staying, do you hear?'

He groaned. 'I'll break your heart. Don't you know that?'

'Yes, and I'll probably break yours. What of it? Hearts break and mend. But if we part again mine will break and never mend.'

She shut off his reply by kissing him. Her embrace held as much strength and determination as passion, and at last the message began to get through to him. The decision was no longer his. She had taken over, imposing her will on him, and all he needed to do was yield in peace and joy.

She drew back, taking his face between her hands. Months of anguish had left him thin and haggard.

'I'm here to stay, do you understand that?' she said. 'No more foolishness; we're going to be married.'

He nodded, smiling faintly.

'If you take me on, it's that lifetime commitment that you didn't want,' he warned her.

'Leave me to worry about that.'

'Evie, listen to me. Once this is done, I won't let you go, ever. I'll be jealous and demanding, possessive, self-ish, unreasonable—'

'That's understood,' she said with a shaky laugh. 'I'll just kick your shins.'

'Be warned. Leave me before it's too late.'

'You fool, it was too late long ago. We just didn't realise it. It's all right.' She kissed him gently. 'It's all right—all right—'

Then he yielded, dropping his head on to her shoulder with a sound that was like a sob. She held him close, soothing him silently.

When he looked up, Hope was standing there in the gloom.

'Did you do this?' he asked.

She nodded.

'Thank you—Mother.' His voice lingered on the word.

Hope gave a little satisfied smile and moved away until she was lost among the trees. They could do without her now, and she had a wedding to plan.

The two in the garden didn't see her go. They had set their feet on a long, troubled road, where there would be bitterness as well as joy. But the joy would be there, all the sweeter for the struggle. And they would travel together, with no turning back.

MILLS & BOON®

Live the emotion

SEPTEMBER 2005 HARDBACK TITLES

ROMANCE™

Title		Code	ISBN
The Disobedient Virgin	*Sandra Marton*	H6244	0 263 18739 X
A Scandalous Marriage	*Miranda Lee*	H6245	0 263 18740 3
Sleeping with a Stranger	*Anne Mather*	H6246	0 263 18741 1
At the Italian's Command	*Cathy Williams*	H6247	0 263 18742 X
Prince's Pleasure	*Carole Mortimer*	H6248	0 263 18743 8
His One-Night Mistress	*Sandra Field*	H6249	0 263 18744 6
The Royal Baby Bargain	*Robyn Donald*	H6250	0 263 18745 4
Back in her Husband's Bed	*Melanie Milburne*		
		H6251	0 263 18746 2
Wife and Mother Forever	*Lucy Gordon*	H6252	0 263 18747 0
Christmas Gift: A Family	*Barbara Hannay*		
		H6253	0 263 18748 9
Mistletoe Marriage	*Jessica Hart*	H6254	0 263 18749 7
Taking on the Boss	*Darcy Maguire*	H6255	0 263 18750 0
To Wed a Sheikh	*Teresa Southwick*	H6256	0 263 18751 9
Major Daddy	*Cara Colter*	H6257	0 263 18752 7
A Child To Call Her Own	*Gill Sanderson*	H6258	0 263 18753 5
Coming Home for Christmas	*Meredith Webber*		
		H6259	0 263 18754 3

HISTORICAL ROMANCE™

Title		Code	ISBN
A Reputable Rake	*Diane Gaston*	H609	0 263 18819 1
Conquest Bride	*Meriel Fuller*	H610	0 263 18820 5
Princess of Fortune	*Miranda Jarrett*	H611	0 263 18949 X

MEDICAL ROMANCE™

Title		Code	ISBN
The Nurse's Christmas Wish	*Sarah Morgan*		
		M525	0 263 18843 4
The Consultant's Christmas Proposal	*Kate Hardy*		
		M526	0 263 18844 2

MILLS & BOON®
Live the emotion

SEPTEMBER 2005 LARGE PRINT TITLES

ROMANCE™

HISTORICAL ROMANCE™

MEDICAL ROMANCE™

0805 Gen Std LP

MILLS & BOON®

Live the emotion

OCTOBER 2005 HARDBACK TITLES

ROMANCE™

Blackmailing the Society Bride *Penny Jordan*		
	H6260	0 263 18755 1
Baby of Shame *Julia James*	H6261	0 263 18756 X
Taken by the Highest Bidder *Jane Porter*	H6262	0 263 18757 8
Virgin for Sale *Susan Stephens*	H6263	0 263 18758 6
The Italian's Convenient Wife *Catherine Spencer*		
	H6264	0 263 18759 4
The Antonakos Marriage *Kate Walker*	H6265	0 263 18760 8
Mistress to a Rich Man *Kathryn Ross*	H6266	0 263 18761 6
Tamed by her Husband *Elizabeth Power*	H6267	0 263 18762 4
A Most Suitable Wife *Jessica Steele*	H6268	0 263 18763 2
In the Arms of the Sheikh *Sophie Weston*	H6269	0 263 18764 0
The Marriage Miracle *Liz Fielding*	H6270	0 263 18765 9
Ordinary Girl, Society Groom *Natasha Oakley*		
	H6271	0 263 18766 7
Christmas Due Date *Moyra Tarling*	H6272	0 263 18767 5
The Billionaire's Wedding Masquerade *Melissa McClone*		
	H6273	0 263 18768 3
The Life Saver *Lilian Darcy*	H6274	0 263 18769 1
The Noble Doctor *Gill Sanderson*	H6275	0 263 18770 5

HISTORICAL ROMANCE™

The Outrageous Debutante *Anne O'Brien*	H612	0 263 18821 3
The Captain's Lady *Margaret McPhee*	H613	0 263 18822 1
Winter Woman *Jenna Kernan*	H614	0 263 18950 3

MEDICAL ROMANCE™

Gift of a Family *Sarah Morgan*	M527	0 263 18845 0
Christmas on the Children's Ward *Carol Marinelli*		
	M528	0 263 18846 9

MILLS & BOON®

Live the emotion

OCTOBER 2005 LARGE PRINT TITLES

ROMANCE™

Married by Arrangement *Lynne Graham*	1807	0 263 18587 7
Pregnancy of Revenge *Jacqueline Baird*	1808	0 263 18588 5
In the Millionaire's Possession *Sara Craven*		
	1809	0 263 18589 3
The One-Night Wife *Sandra Marton*	1810	0 263 18590 7
The Italian's Rightful Bride *Lucy Gordon*	1811	0 263 18591 5
Husband by Request *Rebecca Winters*	1812	0 263 18592 3
Contract To Marry *Nicola Marsh*	1813	0 263 18593 1
The Mirrabrook Marriage *Barbara Hannay*	1814	0 263 18594 X

HISTORICAL ROMANCE™

The Earl and the Pickpocket *Helen Dickson*		
	310	0 263 18509 5
A Knight of Honour *Anne Herries*	311	0 263 18510 9
Saving Sarah *Gail Ranstrom*	312	0 263 18956 2

MEDICAL ROMANCE™

The Doctor's Rescue Mission *Marion Lennox*		
	577	0 263 18479 X
The Latin Surgeon *Laura MacDonald*	578	0 263 18480 3
Dr Cusack's Secret Son *Lucy Clark*	579	0 263 18481 1
Her Surgeon Boss *Abigail Gordon*	580	0 263 18482 X

0905 Gen Std LP